In An Italian Garden

IN AN ITALIAN GARDEN

Stories

ARLENE MACLEOD

Weymouth Press

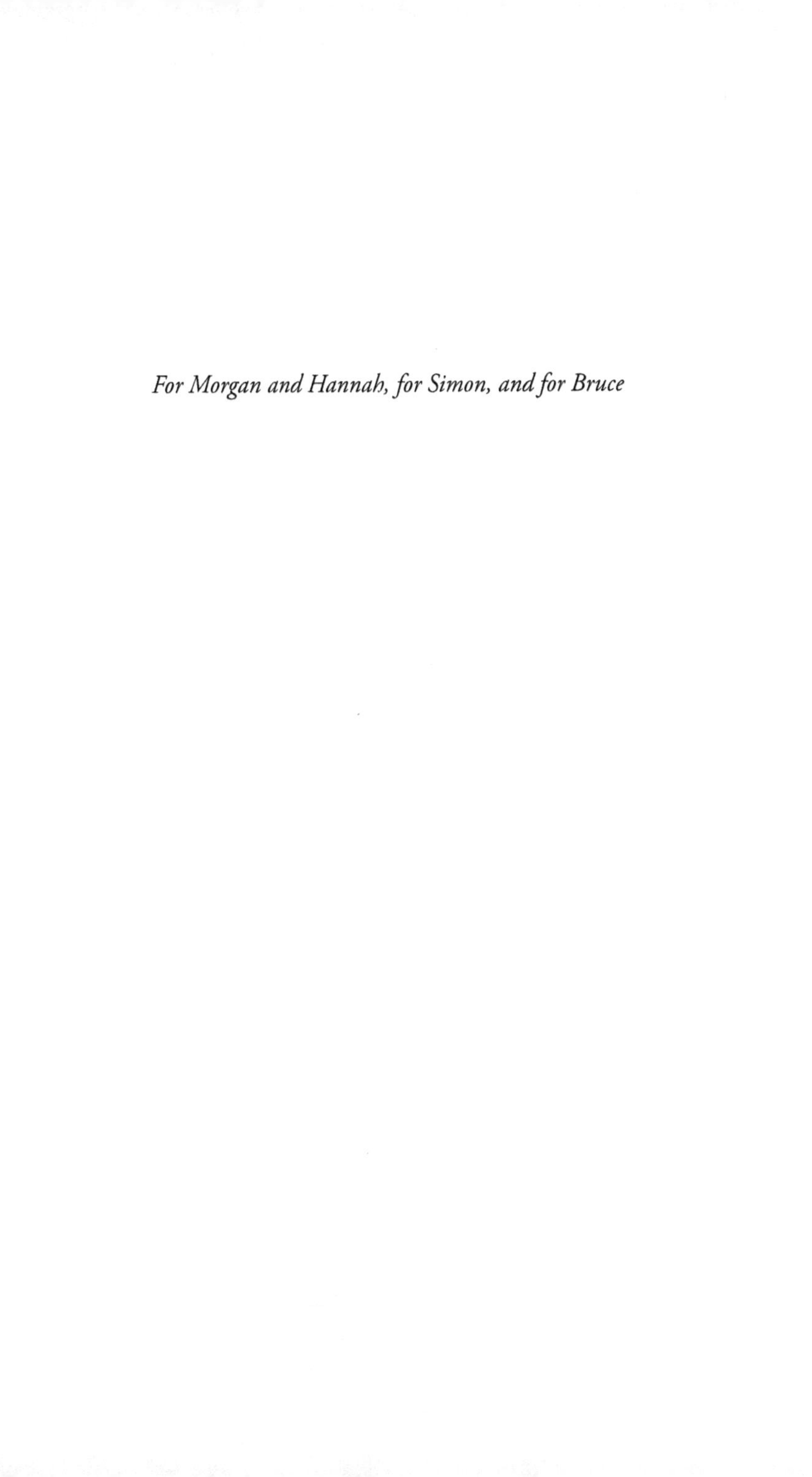

For Morgan and Hannah, for Simon, and for Bruce

CONTENTS

In An Italian Garden

THE SMELL OF ORANGES

The smell of oranges rolled off the lush leaves and round fruits and in the glowing noon sun the plants along the strangely named African Path shimmered like the green water of Lake Maggiore below. Anastasia walked along the gravel path, lined with waist high pots, her fingers just touching the leaves. They felt warm and and left a damp trail along her forearms as they brushed her; they were furry and furled and so alive they seemed aware, as though they were reaching out. But that was exactly the kind of crazy thought she was not supposed to have anymore.

She pulled her fingers away. At the end of the path she found a café with striped umbrellas. She plunked her heavy bag down on a metal table and pulled a chair screeching over the bricks into the shade. At the next table, a man wearing wire glasses grimaced and set his shoulder against her as he picked up his book again. Ass, she thought as she sat. As though there weren't plenty more like him; they packed the halls and pubs of Cambridge, where she'd spent the last ten years teaching, though she was not a Brit. She came from Boston. The old world had always seemed so much finer than the new, but lately she wasn't sure. Still, he couldn't intimidate her. She sat up even more straight on the wobbly chair. She wouldn't let him. But she knew the rage she felt was another symptom.

She picked up the menu but didn't look at it. The sun was warm, she told herself, pleasantly so, and a cool but not chill breeze wafted up from the white-capped lake and tousled her heavy hair, tickling her neck. She brushed her hair back and straightened her shoulders and turned her thoughts. For instance, what a strange place this formal garden was, constructed at enormous cost by hundreds of laborers on a tiny island in the lake. Built in the 1600's to resemble a ship cutting through the waves by a power mad prince, Isola Bella was designed to intimidate and overwhelm, yet still it had these intimate corners where one could imagine lingering, maybe over a glass of wine or a novel; they had those then, didn't they? She wasn't entirely sure. She was no historian. And why was the smell of citrus so entirely pleasurable? That was a question she couldn't answer either. Her discipline was organic chemistry, but on Mars and other possible distant planets. The funders were enthralled with the idea that maybe if certain chemicals existed in just the right amounts, life too would be found. It might be, she had always thought so, but she wondered if humans would even recognize such life; it might be so very different from life experienced here on earth, as in this garden, this body. Like what if the scent of orange was a distasteful odor, or what if aliens didn't have a sense of smell at all, or what if they measured their lives not in these minutes between mealtimes and the pattern of day and night but in multiple centuries; what if they didn't equate life and movement at all? These questions intrigued her, but apparently voicing them at conferences hadn't helped and her colleagues were puzzled at best or seriously annoyed when she leaped over the established lines that indicated their field and started doing what they called speculation or even, she'd heard a whisper about herself, science fiction.

The man at the next table coughed and Anastasia dropped her eyes to the menu. No sense thinking any of these thoughts. She wasn't a chemist anymore, organic or otherwise. She hadn't stayed for the inevitably disappointing decision on promotion to the senior permanent rank. It had seemed better to slink away, just fade from their sight. Only in the process, she'd rather faded from her own view as well. So what she was right now was unclear even to her, hidden, or nebulous, still to be seen. A kind of science fiction actually, or an evolving personal experiment. She tried to think of it that way in her good moments.

And that was why she was here, more or less. Here in the Italian Lakes, in the fantastical island garden of the Borromeos, that wealthy power-seeking Renaissance family. Part of an eight day independent garden tour in Northern Italy. She'd picked up a brochure outside the dean of faculty's office; someone had left it crumpled and creased on the table by the door. Waiting for her terminal interview, she'd examined the tiny crinkled photo of Lake Maggiore, brilliant blue under a hot Italian sun. Eight days to figure it out, she'd thought, eight days to grow like cells in a petrie dish, or coagulate, like salt adhering to a bamboo stick in water, eight days to become coherent, to crystallize and to know who she would be now and after.

It would be sufficient time. It would be enough.

She blinked and wrinkled her nose to stop the urgent prickling behind her eyes. This vacation or interval or whatever it was would be long enough, she would make it work. And here was as good as anywhere else. Better. She made herself look up from the hot metal table. Here, with the school kids pushing and shouting as they raced up and down the granite steps. Here, with the German tourists on walking tours and earnest English gardeners sticking fingers into the soil of the potted limes and bitter oranges. In truth, this particular tiny corner of Earth was extremely pleasant in the noon sun with an orange tree providing dappled shade over her head. And a week of empty days was a long, long time.

The waitress approached, her blonde hair in a bun slipping slightly to the right in an endearing way and her smile real. Anastasia ordered a crepe with marmalade and an espresso, hot water on the side. The waitress noted it down in careful looping script, smiled again, straightened the napkin and fork in front of her, and departed.

"The coffee is too strong, you won't like it at all," said the man at the next table. He peered at her with a frown over his slim serious book, as though she shouldn't have bothered him by ordering it.

Anastasia shrugged and smiled in a hopefully distant manner and took out her own book as a hint. But he wouldn't be put off now.

"These Italians make their coffee too strong, and they put too much olive oil over everything." He gestured to his plate where a half-eaten panini was strewn in unappetizing disarray over the edge of the plate and even onto the table.

Anastasia felt her fingers curl in an urge to pick up the fallen tomatoes. She put her hands in her lap and clasped her fingers together. "Well," she said, but couldn't think how to continue.

He looked at her as though she were useless and returned to his book. She was relieved, but also annoyed. "So why are you here then, if you hate all the food and the coffee and presumably pretty much everything else?" she said.

He put down his book, marked the page with a slip of paper, and shut the cover. "I must be."

"Must?"

"My wife died," he said, "though she wasn't my wife, not actually."

"Oh," Anastasia said. "I'm very sorry." They were both silent for a moment, but she was thinking that he hadn't really answered her question.

He got up, presumably distressed by her insensitivity, threw some euros on the table, and left. Anastasia watched him go, walking fast with a slight limp of his left foot, and wondered about his life and his not wife and death. But excessive curiosity was always her downfall, she remembered, so she took up the menu again and studied it.

When the waitress returned, she looked distressed also, as the euros were insufficient. Feeling some sort of responsibility for the irresponsibility of another English speaking person, Anastasia found herself handing the waitress a ten euro note.

"Oh, grazie, you don't know how hard it is making ends meet. I have a little boy."

"Yes," said Anastasia, wondering when her coffee might come and wishing she could be left alone with it in this hot and fragrant place.

The waitress sat down opposite her. "You know what it is," she said, "how old are your children?"

"Actually, I haven't any," said Anastasia. She wished she had because the waitress looked so disappointed, as though their only possible point of connection had just been severed. She was used to this. Even in academia most people had kids. And when you didn't, they assumed you didn't want them. It made them mad, and uncomfortable, and they made assumptions, that you were selfish or immature or both. "My coffee?" she said gently.

The waitress looked puzzled, then she laughed. "Oh it's cold now I'm sure, I'll have Marco make another." She bustled off, adjusting her white apron over her navy skirt.

But now the scent from the cluster of potted gardenias nearby was suddenly too strong and the glare made her forehead ache. Anastasia got to her feet, swaying, grabbed her bag and slung it over her shoulder, the novels inside clunking against her back. She would go, she would get the very next boat off this overbearing island. She couldn't stay here any longer. It was all too strange and too sad.

She tossed coins onto the table and hurried down the path, lined with orange and yellow poppies bobbing in the breeze she made, waving to her as she passed, but that was another thought she shouldn't be having. Poppies were just annuals or maybe perennials and though they were alive certainly, they weren't alive in any way a person was and shouldn't be given a person's qualities.

That way lay danger. Even though, if one thought about it enough, poppies and people were all just combinations of chemicals.

She turned left, descended a dank stairway flanked with healthy succulents and emerged in the bright sun again, down by the water, breathing hard. She walked past the stalls hawking scarves and baseball hats and lake-view postcards, ignoring the calls of the proprietors, trying to look calm and slow her breathing, and found the ferry, which was about to depart. She boarded and sat on a plastic chair toward the front, in the wind. She imagined the kindly waitress appearing with the crepe and the hot coffee and finding her gone, and she felt bad and half rose from her seat, but it was too late. There was no going back. There never was.

She sat down again, feeling a blush heat her cheeks and she took off her sweater, pretending she was hot. She had to put it on again once they were underway because the breeze was actually quite chilly.

When Anastasia left the ferry and walked ashore at Stresa, she had an awkward two hours and a half before the next train back to Milan. She'd already strolled around the tiny square in the center of town yesterday, purchasing a few notecards with watercolor scenes of the lake framed by cascades of roses. And she'd walked earlier today along the waterfront path, past the various famous old hotels, with their manicured lawns and gingerbread trellises and slightly shabby air. They looked wonderfully elegant in one way, but in another, quite ancient and decayed. And everyone who came out of their opulent carved doors, which wasn't that many people at all, seemed to be at least eighty. More than twice her age. She was thirty-eight, an age when she should be some-where else, employed and needed, maybe wed or a parent, busy at any rate. Not wandering aimless among decaying buildings, overblown beds of pink and white petunias, and slow-strolling amblers hefting canes and examining menus.

She took a turn onto a narrow street that looked like a regular place where regular people lived. She couldn't really get lost here; it was a small town and with the train station on top of the hill and the lake at the bottom, fairly easy to navigate. She passed a news stand plastered with photos of Kate Middleton, the royal newcomer, having a baby, though looking at her flat belly, it certainly didn't show. The garish pictures in every tabloid and cheap magazine showed her, thinner and thinner, smiling more and more. The Italian papers also featured Kate but she was nearly crowded out with pictures of the new pope. The old one hadn't died, but he'd recused himself, as though being a saint was something one could retire from and now a new pope presided, smiling in a cunning yet genial way over massive weeping and cheering crowds.

Anastasia leaned in closer, examining the faces in the crowd, so unguarded in their various emotions, looking for what fueled their exuberance, until the shop owner came out and barked something at her. She shook her head and hurried off down the road. She was lost, that's what it felt like, lost in the middle of a road or a life, not following any expected trajectory.

She walked fast, her bag's straps cutting into her shoulder. At the end of the street, she crossed a busier road, cars screeching to a halt for her, and continued along as the sidewalks disappeared and the road grew more narrow and eventually turned into a parking lot sufficient for three compact cars. Granite stairs led down to the lake and up to the train station and just ahead of her was an abandoned villa, encircled by a rusted iron fence overgrown with vines and some purple flower with an odd smell and a shape like a bell in a church.

She put her bag down on the mossy step and peered into the garden beyond the fence. The vine leaves were soft and felt like velvet to her fingers. She stared into the garden, rubbing the leaves along her palms, and imagined a woman dressed in ancient burgundy velvet, aged like a fine wine to a chocolate brown. The woman wandered among the overgrown plants and arching vines, touching one leaf here and another there with a puzzled look on her face, as though she wasn't sure how she'd found her way here or perhaps why she found her garden in such disarray.

Anastasia leaned in closer and looked.

Then the woman saw her and her grey eyes grew wide and filled with tears. "Is it you again?" she said, walking towards her. "It's been so very long. I've been watching and watching for you."

Anastasia jerked away, the old woman's musky scent mixing with the jasmine winding along the fence post, making her feel sick. She clutched at her stomach, breathing too fast, then picked up her bag and backed away from the gate and hurried down the street. She took the first corner and walked, faster and faster, almost running. It was starting to sprinkle; soon it would rain. Two school children raced each other to an open door. The door gaped open, orange light spilling out and embracing them; they entered and the door shut and the street was grey and rain came down, sliding in cold drops down her back.

Two days later, Anastasia was back in Stresa. She couldn't stay away, though she thought perhaps she should. Certainly she should. Still, she'd found herself knotting a silk scarf with blue tassels around her neck, humming, then walking with purpose down the busy street that led away from her hotel in the center of Milan, with its towering gingerbread cathedral and ornate glass and marble shopping arcades. Walking toward the chunky sandstone castle from another era. She passed its crenelated walls and entered the regional train station. She knew her way around now. It was easy to purchase another ticket from the machine and she knew the correct track and she thought with anticipation of the espresso she'd have in the café across from the ferry station when she reached the town.

But after the train ride, when she reached Stresa, it seemed to be a local holiday of some sort. Her espresso shop was shut, a sign over the door. She stared at the handwritten sign, which she could not read, feeling inexpressibly sad. But she must pull herself together, this was only a small impasse. And there would be so many more. Delays and obstacles and decisions and derailments. That's what life came down to, didn't it? More and more and more. A wave of worry rose up in her chest and she tried to swallow it down.

What holiday was this anyway? The streets were silent and empty even of the school children usually walking in rowdy rows, laden with backpacks, kicking each other when the teacher looked away out over the lake.

Anastasia started to walk, wishing for the dark smell of coffee, but all the shops seemed to be shadowed and shuttered tight. She wandered down one street, and then another, but every street was silent as though all the inhabitants had fled.

She thought of the woman in velvet then, in the abandoned garden with its crumbling villa, windows covered with wrought iron tracery overgrown with falls of wisteria. But she had promised herself, back in Milan, that she was not returning to Stresa for that.

She had paused in front of a shop without realizing, and in her first good fortune of the day, she saw that it was a bike shop, its wide door propped open. Red bikes leaned against a rack, available to rent for the day. The owner, a plump middle-aged woman, like herself but comfortable in her skin, fitted her on a heavy hybrid and handed her a well-used helmet, a new water bottle, and a faint copy of a map, then went back inside without speaking at all. Anastasia heard the rapid fire Italian of the television and then the door clunked shut.

She wheeled the heavy bike along the cobbled street, past the postcard stands, toward the wide avenue by the water, feeling pleased and proud. Maybe she'd go for a ride along the lake. Peter would have pushed her to ride all the way around the lake, miles and miles, up and down Alps, into Switzerland and back. He'd have done it himself, as a small adventure. But he wasn't here, he was back in the U.K., where she no longer lived, and anyway he'd made it clear six months ago that he wasn't interested. It was the one very good thing about never going back to Cambridge, she wouldn't have to see him again. He'd liked his name to be pronounced Pet-er, in a vaguely Scandinavian way, and sometimes in the nights she dreamed of handwritten letters, cascades of them, piling up inside the door of her old flat, under the mail slot. But when she tried to lean in and read the return address she could never tell where he was when he'd written, and when she tried to open a letter it fell apart in her fingers and she could never find out what he'd said.

She frowned and remembered she was not going to care about that anymore. She got on the bike and concentrated on pushing the heavy pedals around. The first revolution was hard but it grew easier. She cycled on, and grew warm, and the sun peered out from behind purple clouds. There was some famous inn, she remembered from the guidebook, and if she got there she could get coffee and view their gardens, a perfectly respectable day of a normal tourist.

After riding about four kilometers along the lake, her legs getting rubbery from the heavy bike, she found the inn. But the black iron gate was shut and padlocked. She sat down on a curb beside the gate and examined the creeping rosemary with its blue flowers trailing along the stone. She fingered the stiff delicate flowers and sighed and thought again about the old woman in her faded velvet in the neglected garden. Hadn't she seemed like she might have something to say?

To distract herself, she stared out over the lake, lit one moment by the sun and purple the next as clouds shifted over. In the distance, mountains rose white-topped and silent. The ice gleamed against the purple piling clouds, and she wanted to put a finger out and stroke the softness of the snow. A discarded glass bottle rattled down the street and lodged against the curb by her foot. She shook her head to clear it and stood up.

She wheeled the bike along the street of a tiny town. Shops were opening now and a church bell was ringing and people were coming out of their homes in festive clothes. Seeing them and hearing laughter and children's high voices, she felt her own mood lift. Perhaps there would even be coffee.

A bright sign, swinging and creaking on a chain in the wind off the lake, stopped her. The sign showed a half moon painting, a lunette of a Medici garden and villa. Below, in fanciful green script, the sign proclaimed, "Lessons in Painting" in English and again in French and at the very bottom, in Italian.

Anastasia studied the shop window, which displayed a palette, three round-tip sable brushes with short handles, and an opened book showing the famous statue from the Borromeo's garden, the one of the unicorn ridden by proud Eros. Perhaps it would be engrossing, perhaps it would keep her mind where it ought to be, in the present, looking toward the future.

She leaned the bike against the stone wall and stepped down three stairs into the dark shop. Cold air swirled around her neck and chilled her bare arms. It smelled of linseed oil and paint. A boy slouched on a stool in the corner. "I'm here about the lessons," Anastasia said slowly, pointing behind her to the sign.

"My sister does that. She's not here."

His English was fine with an accent that was somewhat British. "I see. When will she be back?"

The boy shrugged and got to his feet. He was tall and lean, like a runner, and a heavy silver bracelet clunked on his wrist.

"I want to paint a lunette, like the one you have out front. When are the lessons?"

"You don't need a lesson for that. Anyone can do it," he said and picked up a brush.

There was a long table behind him, she saw now, lit by a single light bulb swinging on a cord from a low beam, and covered with stacks of wood panels, glasses filled with paintbrushes, pencils and rulers, and half-squeezed tubes of paint.

"Not anyone," Anastasia said, lacing her fingers behind her back. "Teach me." He hesitated and she wondered if she should offer him money or at least ask what it would cost her.

"All right." He picked up a pencil, examined the point, and handed it to her.

"Now?"

"You want to learn?"

She sat down and the boy rolled up his sleeves carefully, so she pulled hers up too and flipped the tasseled scarf out of the way behind her back. He squeezed six colors of paint on a wood palette and handed it to her. She grasped the palette, surprised by its weight, and smelled the strong chemical odor of the paints. The colors were bright daubs on the scraped wood. When she picked up the brush, it felt exactly right in her fingers. She smiled at the boy.

He ignored that and showed her how to divide the panel into quadrants and create a grid and how to measure off the diagonal lines for keeping the proper perspective. He handed her a wrinkled print of one of Utens' paintings, the lunette of the Medici villa at Castello.

"You must draw in the outlines of the various garden rooms first, in pencil," he said. "The correct symmetry is all important." He watched her sketch in the orchard rooms and the central fountain area and then, apparently satisfied, he left her alone while she continued. He returned with an espresso for each of them and she tossed it down, as he did, and then he showed her how to mix the colors but it seemed as though she knew what he would say as he said it and gradually he forgot to tell her anything and became absorbed in his own painting and she was free to contemplate hers. She was glad she was doing a Medici garden, not the terraced baroque splendor of the Borromeos, but a satisfyingly geometrical and orderly Renaissance garden, with parterres and citrus trees in pots, and fountains whose leaping water mimicked the flow of leaves in the olive orchards in the hot winds.

They painted together all afternoon.

"You've painted before," he said, when he finally put down his brushes and looked over her shoulder.

"Yes," she said, "though not for a very long time." So long that she'd almost forgotten that once she'd dreamed of being an artist, of seeing the world in colors and shapes and spending her days really looking.

"You'd best go back, it's going dark," he said. "Come earlier tomorrow."

Back in Stresa, the woman at the bike shop was grumpy when she counted out the money as she'd interrupted the evening aperitivo, but she rented the bike again for the next day, and walked up the granite stairs to the train, thinking about her lunette and the mossy green and deep copper she was using to paint the trees and she was so engrossed that she almost passed the deserted villa without realizing.

She hesitated by the rusted fence and hooked a finger daubed with green paint around the cold iron. She could hear small birds flitting and rustling in the overgrown ivy. A huge butterfly, lavender-blue and black, landed on the tall stem of an iris and rested there, like an even more exotic flower. There was another sound, Anastasia thought, or was there? She would look, for a moment only, within. She pushed aside the damp trailers of jasmine, and it seemed at first that there was only dusk shrouding a dark and neglected garden. But then the old woman appeared from behind the citrus trees and came right towards her, with something urgent in her face and agitated gait.

Anastasia felt the breath knocked from her chest, as though she'd fallen or had an electric shock, and she stepped back quickly, back through the gate and onto the sidewalk and right into a passing man, who apologized, thought it was clearly her fault. When he'd gone on and she looked back into the garden, it was empty and already dark, as it would be, of course.

For three more days Anastasia came to Stresa, picked up the clunky bike, rode the four kilometers, and sat down to paint. The boy painted too. He was fast and he'd completed one lunette already and started another. He sold them to tourists, he told her. He also told her his name was Michele. His sister never came by but that didn't matter to Anastasia and they painted, most of the time, in silence.

She was completely absorbed in her lunette, the silvery leaves and deep shadows enclosed by pleasing geometry. There was something she seemed to know already about the intricate shapes and the overall design of foliage, which was her favorite part to paint. She was pleased that a lunette is a view from above and afar; she could simply ignore the details of flowers and stick to the pleasing forms of topiary— spiraling cedars, balls of eglantine, cones of fir. She knew the chemistry and composition of plants, perhaps that was it. Their unique kind of life that was life but yet so different from the life we know. As she painted the olive and apricot orchards, she thought about how these plants must surely speak to each other, in small directional changes of their leaves or a caress of one branch to another in a soft and convenient breeze. Perhaps, with true attention, love could be found anywhere, in some yet unrecognized form, and not just in the complications of people.

On the third afternoon she finished. It would be a crime to put more paint on the lunette; it had reached its end. And with the ending came a wash of panic in her throat. She had only one day left of the eight days of her independent tour and what had she decided? Where could her life go next?

"You could start another," said Michele, his brush poised, a crease between his eyebrows. "I will charge you only half price for the next."

"Where is your sister?"

"In the hospital," he said. "My apologies. She is a better teacher. I have to wait here until she can come back."

"I'm so sorry," said Anastasia. "She is very ill?"

"I was supposed to leave for university a month ago. I'm studying to be an engineer."

"But you have such a talent for painting," she said.

He shrugged. "That's what everyone says. Especially my mother."

"What would you build?"

"Bridges." He gestured to the lunettes, laid out in rows of six on the table.

And when she looked, she saw that he'd painted a tiny bridge in the background of each garden scene. Wooden bridges, arching bridges, stone bridges, long filigreed spans and one with a horse and rider galloping across.

"I see," she said. "Then I wish you good luck and health to your sister."

"My sister is the painter," he said as he wiped his brush.

Anastasia cycled back to town slowly, the painting strapped on her back; the oil paint would be wet for days yet. But that was good, she thought as she pedaled. She could dream some more about the underside of the olive leaves, consider how to get that exact shade of green, or was it actually silver? Think about the mysterious world she'd created on a panel of wood.

She turned in the bike and carried the painting down an empty side street so it wouldn't be gawked at or brushed by tourists hurrying on. She didn't think about it, but the street brought her to the neglected villa.

Anastasia smelled the old woman's musky perfume already as she stepped through the gate and up onto the granite block in the center of the overgrown garden and waited. She lifted her own hand to her nose and smelled the same musky scent mixed now with the sharpness of oil paint and turpentine. Her mind felt cloudy and odd, perhaps from the fumes or maybe the heat. It was warm, so very warm and so humid, as though the water rose in a thick mist from the oval droplets scattered over all the pale drooping roses and furry leaves and bent stalks of grass.

The painting felt heavy and dragged against her shoulder, so she moved the jasmine vine aside and propped it carefully against the metal fence. When she returned to the granite block, the old woman was there already, sitting quietly, her head cocked to the side as though waiting for her and listening.

Anastasia shook her head, feeling the familiar cloudy sloshy strangeness behind her eyes. She sat down beside the old woman. "Peter left. And my work is gone, I've lost my job forever, and well, it's all gone now, everything that I was."

"Yes," said the woman, avoiding her eyes. "But you could come back now, with me, to your old home."

"I have only just gotten away! I am well now, how can you even suggest it?" Anastasia got to her feet.

"What will you do then, how can you live?" The woman lifted her two hands, palms upward, and the question hung in the air. "Anyone can live, just surviving." She pointed to the unkempt sprawl of the garden at their feet. "The plants know the difference." She put out a hand, pale in the dim light with nails rimmed with earth from the gardens and her voice turned low and cajoling. "You should stay here, with me. I'm lonely too, you know."

Anastasia felt her heart skip a few beats, as though it was wondering whether to keep on. What would it be like to have a mother, a sister, a daughter, or a lover, another woman to be a companion of the heart? She closed her eyes, and smelled the dark air of the garden's lush growing, her chest tight.

Then she coughed and straightened her shoulders and made herself look away. She picked up her wood panel and held her lunette at arm's length and studied the intricate patterns until her shoulders ached. She hefted the painting onto her back and walked away, not looking back.

After the train ride, back in Milan, she'd take a long hot shower in her blank hotel room and then she'd go out for an evening stroll among the families, all of them strolling along the fragrant garden walkways, all the generations together. She would sit like the others in a sidewalk cafe and hold an icy goblet in her fingers. She was separated from her past, ignorant of her future. But she was a human and she would act like one.

ON THE EVE

The north of Italy, 1915

Anna did not like lakes; they gave off a watery dismal smell that make her think disconsolate lonely thoughts. And it was a strange spring of drifting mists and a pale white round of sun barely visible, providing no warmth or brightness at all. She stood at the edge of the lake, gazing out, a child, her child, clinging to her knees. They'd come a long way, leaving her parents' home, traveling with her new husband through Berlin and Munich in the dark autumn of 1914, and once spring came, trudging alongside a cart up the muddy track through the Alps.

It was still unseasonably cold, buds coiled tight on the trees. Anna shifted Catrin's hand and pulled a pencil and crumpled paper from her pocket. She looked at the words she'd written: dim, granite, dank, desolate, grime. Her attempts at poems here were as gloomy and murky as those she'd written at the table by the hearth on the farm where she'd grown up. The family home in

Skane had been drowned in winter rain and dark lakes and she'd left it far behind when she accepted Louis' unexpected proposal, just as she'd passed thirty, a widow with a child who'd thought that part of her life was over. She'd followed him, grateful and full of newly acquired hope, through Germany and Austria-Hungary and, in the first rush of spring, on into Italy. Louis had coaxed her through this strange winter of hard travel, with frightening news of the war on every corner, charmed her with drawn out tales of sand beaches and warm breezes that caressed your bare skin. They had sipped clove-spiced red wine and clung to each other in their canvas tent when Catrin had gone to sleep, obliterating any troubles of the day, reveling in their bodies insisting on each other.

But now, instead of the promised Mediterranean sun beating on her coiled braids, there was only this chill wind. They'd stopped, barely over the Italian border, in a small unfriendly town on the edge of Lago di Como, home to a famed villa and its trampled and forgotten gardens, remarkable for little else. They'd halted here and when she'd asked Louis why, he said only, "I have to join the fighting."

Catrin interrupted Anna's complaining thoughts, bumping into her knees and falling crying at her feet. Anna picked up her daughter, feeling her small heart pumping and her plump arms hot with her exuberant and overdone emotions. "Never mind," she said, patting her back and smoothing down her springy curls. She carried her to the wicker garden chair propped by the iron garden gate and pulled Catrin onto her lap. She said something like this twenty times a day to Catrin, but it never moderated her daughter's feelings.

"He meant what he said," said Catrin, following her words with a loud wail.

"Hush," said Anna. "Hush now, I'm sure he didn't." Her eyes met Dickon's. He was standing with arms crossed over his chest and a sullen narrowing of his ridiculously lovely, for a boy, green eyes. Dickon was the son of the English head gardener and his Italian wife, and he was eleven, twice Catrin's age. She idolized him, trailing after him and annoying him, surely, all the time. Yet he tolerated her, for the most part.

"I'm off to help my dad, manuring the roses," Dickon said now. "I've no choice in the matter."

Catrin burst into fresh cries.

Anna got to her feet, stumbling forward with the still surprising weight of her belly. She was five months gone and what she really wanted, she sometimes thought, was to bake like a sponge cake in an oven. Just slowly growing warmer and warmer and crisping slightly around the edges. She was cold and tired all the time, lugging her body around, taking care of Catrin, and how she'd manage when the new baby came, with Louis away, she didn't know. He'd promised her a nanny or a nurse, but the girl he'd sent round before he left was insolent and her olive skin above her low bodice was so very smooth that Anna herself imagined running a cool finger over the top of that rounded breast. No, she didn't think having this girl, Rafaela or whatever her name was, was a solution for anything at all.

A week later, Anna lingered by the lake, Catrin flung in sleep beside her on the grass. The sun was peeking in and out of swift passing clouds and the lake rushed purple below the high, snow-crowned mountains. Anna dipped a hand into the water and swished her fingers back and forth. The water felt thick and heavy and smelled as though a fish had just been caught.

Dickon appeared at her elbow. He was always doing that, catching her off guard. He sat down on the grass, equally distant from Catrin and herself, making a precise triangle. "I can't do it, you know I can't," he said.

"Or you won't. It's all the same, isn't it," said Anna. Her head ached. She knew he'd weasel out in the end. He'd promised to help her, when they first arrived, if it was required. He'd do anything, he'd said. He'd have done anything for Louis, but not, it seemed, for her.

"It's wrong, it's stealing. I'd be put in jail in the city," said Dickon. "What would my father do then? There would be no one to help him, with Albert gone to join up." Albert was his older brother. He was silent a moment, his fingers shredding the grass. Then he said in a low tone she could hardly catch, "I couldn't bear that."

"Never mind," said Anna, her annoyance fading. He was only a child after all. It was just that she was so alone, with Louis gone, and nothing seemed to have fallen out as she'd expected. How Louis' blue eyes had flashed when he spoke of the war coming and his duty and even she'd been drawn in, mesmerized as always by his fascinating French accent. It had all seemed so romantic and adventurous, and she'd been so ready to leave her dark family home with its clouded windows and her shabby village so quenched in the mid-autumn pale light. And leave her life also, stuck on the farm with her aged parents and her child. She'd grasped at the chance in truth, informed her brother that he and his lazy wife must care for their parents now; her turn was done. And the travel, though arduous, had been just as adventurous and romantic as she'd dreamed. But now the war she'd hardly believed in had come, and promised to set in and lengthen. Louis had talked more, on and on about duty, his eyes off on something far away and not on her, and then one morning he was gone.

And she had no one to rely on but herself. She stared at the wrinkles crawling on the surface of the lake. "It's alright, I suppose. I'll think of another way."

"You can't go doing it yourself," said the boy, flicking a quick glance at her belly. His nose turned pink and he looked away.

"I can do more than you think," said Anna. "More than a boy like you could ever know."

He looked at her with his steady eyes, so green and clear, until she felt ashamed for her antipathy. It wasn't directed at him.

"Maybe," he said and slipped away through the cedar hedge, releasing the green scent into the foggy chill air.

She'd have to take Catrin with her; there was no other way. There was no one else to look after her, even for a couple of hours, and besides if anything went wrong, she could make up something about the child and no doubt Catrin would scream and carry on and that would complicate matters enough that they'd get away. Another whole month in the dismal village on the edge of Lake Como had passed, an endless month of dank, not yet spring days. It was just before dawn on a cloudy morning with a fierce wind blowing the olive leaves inside out and silver on the trees. The lake was rutted with grey waves.

Anna dressed in a rush, shivering, and threw a wool shawl over her head and shoulders. She laced up heavy walking boots and dumped their few clothes into her traveling bag. From the chest under the bed, she took the pistol Louis had given her before he left. Just in case, he'd said. She stuck it in her sash, at the back of her waist. Then she went to wake Catrin.

"No," said Catrin, batting her hand away and squinting her eyes shut.

"I haven't time for a tantrum," said Anna. "Get these clothes on, now." For once Catrin seemed too sleepy to protest. She tugged on her long stockings and pulled on her gown and Anna tied her bonnet strings tight under her chin.

"That hurts," said Catrin, her eyes filling. Anna looked away from the blue eyes, so like Louis' that people mistook Catrin for his own. She hadn't heard from Louis in three long months and there was no more time to waste or to hope. If I don't return, he'd said, or if I don't at least write, take the money from the old man and go. You must do it, Anna. Much depends on this, the lives of many good men, and if I can't finish the task myself, you must go to Paris and deliver the message to Jean Chanzy, on Rue Antoine. And then you must go north again, you must save yourself and our child. He had placed a hand on her belly, his palm warm and gentle. She had hugged him tight to her even as he spoke, denying the words, barely listening, thinking of warmth and summer and traveling together on his return, further and further south. Their child would be born in the sun.

But all the long nights of this endless spring, as the war came closer, his words swirled and repeated in her head, keeping her awake, making her cranky with Catrin over their breakfast of hard brown rolls and coffee. She had to do it, now, before the soldiers everyone in town spoke of arrived, before her time was on her. Yesterday, in the café, she'd heard the Austrians were lodged in the mountains, prepared for fighting, already. The Italians were massing near Lago di Garda. And from the twinges and kicks in her body, she knew. There was no more time. But what would it be like, to be a kind of thief? What would she be like, after?

Catrin shuffled behind her, down the stairs, their boots clumping too loud. On the landing, Anna took Catrin's hand and they descended to the bottom floor. It was quiet, the rich old man who rented out her lodgings still sleeping and even his three servants not about. She had watched them morning after morning to learn their routines and she took a quick breath, feeling a strange kind of pride at her success.

"Mama," said Catrin loudly, squeezing her hand. "Mama, I'm hungry."

"Hush," said Anna. "We'll eat after."

"After what? After what?" repeated Catrin, when she didn't reply.

Anna tugged her along, wishing she had endless patience with the child, but she didn't, all her patience had evaporated, gone up into the mist and clouds with this war and her fears. And in truth, Louis was the patient one.

They went into the empty kitchen, the hearth cold and smelling of old ashes. The old cook had let the fire go out again. Anna opened the pantry door and she took two full loaves of bread, and the half loaf left over, though it was stale. She took a chunk of cheese and six wizened apples and thrust them in her bag. She took a bottle and filled it with water too, though it hardly seemed necessary with the entire lake in front of them. Catrin trailed after her, confused and for once quiet.

They went back down the long dark hall and Anna took Catrin's arm and pushed her into a small room used as a study and lined with old books. It smelled of dust and leather and stale air. "Here," she whispered, "sit here and wait for me. Do not stir from that chair, do not go anywhere, do you hear me?"

"I hear you," said Catrin in a small voice, curling up.

She'd probably go back to sleep. Anna watched her daughter for a moment, feeling an ache under her ribs at leaving her unwatched, even for a short time, but there was no way around it, she'd been through the plan in her mind so many times and it would be fine. It would all be fine. For a moment only she closed her eyes and imagined herself and Louis and Catrin after, walking up a long grassy hill in the sun, reaching the top together, and gazing on a bright ocean, sparkling and green. A sea of the south, nothing like these grey inland lakes.

She edged the door shut and lifting her skirts so they wouldn't rustle, she passed down the hall until she waited outside a closed door made of walnut, latched tight with brass fittings. She waited, in the shadows, until it seemed like she dissolved and became a kind of shadow in the dark hall herself. She stood there so long she swayed at times, a vertigo of stillness.

Finally, she heard a click and a thud inside the room. The old man was getting up. She stepped back farther into the shadows. He must surely sense her, standing there, and she tried to erase even her thoughts and feelings so that she emanated nothing human, no more than the sad oil painting on the wall, of drooping flowers and hazelnuts and one wine colored leaf, curled at the edges and frilled with decay. She became so still that when the thumping increased and the door was flung open, she was unprepared and almost gasped.

She bit down on her tongue.

The old man's ebony and silver cane proceeded him out of the room. He was wearing a midnight silk dressing gown and his narrow bony calves above his grey slippers were dreadful in their skinny intensity, the veins standing out with the effort of walking. He breathed and gasped so hard at the effort of haltingly progressing down the hall that she doubted he'd hear her even if she did make some sound. But she did not.

He stopped, right in front of the study door. Anna swallowed and rose on her toes, her mind flashing wildly from one plan to another, but then he clumped by the room where Catrin slept and turned the corner and even the sound of his footsteps and cane tap was gone.

She took in a long uneven breath. What would she have done if he'd opened the door? She thought of the dolls Catrin kept clutched in her fingers as she slept each night, wooden dolls from St. Petersburg, Louis had said when he'd given them to her, gaily painted in bright red and yellow. The largest opened onto another smaller doll and another and another, until finally one reached the baby doll, hidden under the layers and sleeping peacefully. Only Catrin had lost the baby in the cedar maze. Anna swallowed and shook her head to clear out the useless thoughts.

The bedroom door stood wide open. Anna slipped inside. The smell of vinegar and stale piss enveloped her so that she instantly wished she could bathe. She was breathing too fast. She slowed her breath and looked around the dim room, wishing she'd dared a light. The bed was huge and canopied, the linen sheets in a tangle and a blanket slid half onto the floor. She almost bent to tidy it up but made herself step past the heaped bed and move toward the window. There was a small chestnut wood dresser, with a mirror and silvered shaving things that gleamed with an evil light. She had to hurry. If she was going to do this. But of course she was. She must. Men would die, Louis had said. You must not fail us.

But what about her dream, of sitting in the hot sun at a café table, chewing on a pencil, writing a poem of her own. Louis had promised her a new life. You have a new life, she chided herself. She must find strength hidden somewhere inside herself, for Catrin, for the new baby. For Louis. Surely she'd find him again, in Paris maybe, when this dreadful useless war was done. Why hadn't they made a better plan?

She tried the top dresser drawer. It was locked. Fingers shaking, she pulled out the long, old-fashioned key Louis had given her from the string around her neck and fitted it into the lock. It caught at first, but then she jiggled it and shifted something and the key turned. She turned too to stare at the gaping door, wide open to the hall, but no one stood there to watch her.

She slid the drawer open. It stuck, with the humidity, but she rattled it, despite the noise, and it opened just enough. She slid a hand inside and her fingers closed on it, right away, a smooth leather notebook bound with a ribbon of silk. She pulled the notebook out. It was exactly as Louis had described, black with a red ribbon. She was tempted to open it. Louis hadn't said what it contained. Lists, she imagined, names. The old man owned a factory near Milan, perhaps he sold steel, or guns, or machines of some sort, suddenly of value in this war. But she must hurry, she couldn't be found here. She stuffed the notebook in the purse hanging from her sash. She reached her hand in the drawer again and groped around. She felt paper and something made of cold glass and in the back she found an envelope. She pulled it out. It was thick and sealed with wax. The banknotes. She stuffed that in her purse as well. Then she shut the drawer and locked it.

She slipped out of the room and bent over Catrin snoring softly curled on the chair. "Wake up chickadee, we need to be going," she whispered and picked up the heavy child. They went down the stairs and Anna's stomach growled at the smell of boiling coffee. She heard the old man talking with the cook in the kitchen. Catrin lifted her head from Anna's shoulder. "Hush," said Anna and Catrin pinched her arm. They fled across the damp stones of the courtyard and entered the garden maze through the west gate with its iron spikes.

Anna put Catrin down. "You'll have to walk now," she said. "I can't carry you anymore." Her chest felt tight.

"Did you do it then?" said a voice. Dickon came around the corner, hedge shears dangling from his hand.

"What's that to you one way or the other?" said Anna. "You weren't man enough." She knew it was cruel but it was all up to her. Men played at war, but she was the one taking the risks, responsible for Catrin and the unborn child too. Tears burned the back of her eyes, but she ignored them and pulled Catrin along, her mind already on the train and the problem of getting Catrin and their three bags on board. No one in this town would help her. They despised her, a woman alone, without husband or family.

Dickon stepped in front of her. "I can't let you do it, you know that," he said. "I can't let you leave."

"Don't be ridiculous," said Anna. But when she looked at Dickon he seemed taller and broader in the shoulders than before. His eyes were wary, narrowed against the sun coming up over the garden wall.

Another boy came around the corner, with Dickon's green eyes and waving black hair, but he was bigger, nearly a man. "I brought my brother," said Dickon. "He's come home before he goes to the front." He shook his head and shrugged. "I had to tell him."

"You'd do this, to her?" Anna pointed at Catrin, standing open mouthed by her side.

"I have to. It's war now, the Austrians have fired on us. Italy has joined the war," said Dickon. "And they won't hurt you, a woman and child, just send you home."

But Anna could see from the tightness of his clenched fists that even he knew that wasn't true. She was a stranger here, a foreigner from the north. If they found the banknotes and the notebook in her purse, they might hang her as a spy. Certainly they'd throw her in their prison. And Catrin, what would they do with her? What would happen to her then?

"You don't have to," said Anna. "No one ever has to. And if you do, you'll remember, all of your life. What you've done. It will haunt you." Even as she cursed the boy, for a moment, she could almost feel sorrow for him.

Dickon stared at her, his eyes wide, then shrugged again and looked away. "It's war now," he repeated. "It's come here to us, just as they said it would."

Suddenly he looked like the man he would become, one more

man among the many, like any other soldier. She wondered why she'd thought he was different. What did this child think he knew about war? Already she and Catrin had seen the rotting bodies, by their dozens, lying in the mud. She would never forget the smell and Catrin would not speak of it. But it must be there somewhere, buried deep under the layers in her head. The bodies, the sloshing water filled pits, and the rats she had killed with rocks.

The brother moved in two steps closer. "Give it to me," he said, putting out his hand, grimy with dirt and streaked with blood from the rose thorns.

"What?" said Anna.

"Give it over," said the brother, shoving aside his leather jacket to show a long unsheathed knife stuck through his belt. "The Austrians are in the mountains. I know you've got something important off the old man. Give it over, or I'll…"

"You'll what," said Anna. She pointed to the badge pinned to his jacket. "You think joining up makes you a man?"

The brother drew his knife and suddenly he reached for Catrin and yanked her from Anna's side, pulling the child along by her loose hair.

"Mama," screamed Catrin.

"Silent," threatened the brother and jerked her hair. Catrin fell to her knees.

"No," said Dickon and put his hand on his brother's arm.

For a moment, they all froze, even the child.

Dickon's fingers, Anna thought, as they'd touched the white lilies in the lakeside garden and stroked Catrin's pink cheeks as they played together in the sun, how very gentle those fingers had been. If only, she thought, if only Louis had not left them, distracted by honor and duty, abandoned them really, or perhaps he'd died. If only the war wouldn't follow them from those dark German valleys to these pristine mountains and men wouldn't die slowly in the thousands in the filthy ice. She saw what would surely come, the blood on the white snow, avalanches crashing, tossing men and burying them alive, and the silence of after the battle, eerie and broken only by ice cracking and wind wailing over the dark lakes.

But imagining a future without this war was useless. There was only her. She couldn't let him take Catrin or herself back to the big house, nor pull the black notebook and the banknotes from her bag, no matter how sorrowful she felt or what she thought she understood.

The brother shoved Dickon away. He fell to his side onto the ground and Anna heard him grunt with pain and she smelled the damp disturbed grass. Catrin's eyes were wide and staring and the brother tightened his grip on her small arm. Anna heard the bone crack. She drew the pistol from her sash. Dickon's eyes grew wide and green as the flowing grass and the broken cedar branches and she took a deep breath and held the air in and aimed. She shot the brother high in his chest and he sank down wordless and Catrin cried out and Dickon yelled and came at her. She shot him in the thigh. He looked at her, surprised, and fell over his brother in a sprawl of limbs, blood leaking onto the grass.

Catrin shouted "Dickon! Dickon!" and nothing would ever be the same, not for him, not for Catrin, not for her, not for the whole world, teetering on the edge. Anna tore off her sash and tied up Dickon's leg. He would live. He would not fight in this war.

She picked up Catrin and turned away, ignoring Dickon's

shouts, ignoring the old man with his raised fist at the door of his house. She walked into the woods, onto the fragrant cedar path that led to the train, in her mind already boarding the last car with its cargo of spring lambs. It would be warm. No one would search for them there. Catrin would be amused and quiet. They would make it to Paris. They would endure. However altered, by all that lay hidden inside.

THE GRAND TOUR

On the Continent, 1758

If she kept quiet and did the washing, they might let her come along. That had been the advice of Ned, her twin, and though Ned was often slow-witted, in this he'd been correct. Also, she was the only one among them who actually knew some Latin and Greek, but that probably wouldn't have mattered. It had seemed impossible for so very long, but then the improbable had happened. "You may make yourself useful," her uncle had said, over the dinner when she'd finally convinced him.

Madeleine crossed the cramped room on the second floor of the inn where they'd halted for the night and gazed on her three sleeping brothers, noticing that Sam, the youngest at only eight, was snoring again and Rob, only a year older, had not removed his shoes.

It was morning and bright sun had lifted over the Alps, streaming into the disheveled room in the recommended but dingy inn, lighting up the tossed cloaks and muddy boots strewn over the floor. Madeleine went to the door and peeked out. Seeing no one, she descended the steep stairs, crossed the empty room below, and walked out into the dazzling day. She shouldn't be out unaccompanied of course, even if they were at home, and here in this foreign place, she could only imagine what her aunt would say about a young unmarried woman walking out alone. But she was twenty-seven, no longer so young, in truth. And Aunt Susan and Uncle Gerald were not here. Miraculously, she was in charge, along with Ned of course, and she just couldn't wait for her brothers to wake, not while sun flickered over alpine primroses and she could hear the far off shouts of the carters. She lifted a hand to shield her eyes from the brightness. In the distance, a line of salt-laden wagons on Stockalper's road rumbled and jolted along, heading over and through the Alps and beyond.

Yesterday they'd climbed the foothills, heading ever upward toward Simplon Pass, the carter taking the coach apart at noon piece by piece and the men sullenly climbing, laden with long wood boards and iron clad wheels. Her brothers had jabbered and capered and ignored the men's grunts and scowls as well as the views, but she'd trudged upward, silent, breathing the winey air, feeling she'd somehow been freed. She'd kept her eyes down and the knowledge her own, even from Ned, always at her side. Now, finally, they were actually over the border. They had entered Italy at long last. It was a mystery that her brothers could bear to sleep such a morning away.

Madeleine strolled down the narrow street of the village, which was called Gondo, her skirts sweeping against unfamiliar silvery plants sprawling over the pavement and spilling from blue ceramic pots. In the town square, small boys were shouting, selling something that looked like a hot pie. She gave the loudest boy one of the strange silver coins and he laughed and handed her four pies, stacked on paper. They steamed in her hand. She tasted saffron and something sweet, apricots maybe, or raisins. Everything was strange here and wonderful and she thought how incredible it was she'd persuaded her uncle that she must come with her brothers on their Tour. It hadn't been easy; she'd worked at it over long dinners and on country walks for months until he'd given in. And Ned had helped; he'd thrown in a word here and there, saying she could do some of the routine housekeeping chores and thus save them money; she could even help with the journals and sketching. She was unquestionably the best amongst them at that. And she was the practical responsible twin, there was that fact; no one would call Ned responsible though he was the man.

Madeleine yawned thinking of the hour she'd spent at midnight, as her brothers slept. She'd worked with one dim candle to see by, sketching their journey upwards to the Pass. Trying to capture something of the surprise of the overbearing mountains and glorious piling clouds. Something to keep as a record of their trip, a souvenir to show curious neighbors when they visited, proving how much the boys had learned from their foreign travels. A proof of her uncle's rising status in their village and London even. And what did a little lost sleep matter to her. She was truly here, in Italy, land of artists and philosophers, seat of all culture and learning. Soon they would descend the mountains and enter the wide fertile plains and then she would see it all.

When Madeleine returned to their inn, saving three of the pies for her brothers, they were awake and groaning, rubbing their heads, which ached, no doubt, with last night's red wine. "Today," she announced, "we'll go on toward the lakes. The Roman, Pliny the younger, had a villa on the shores of Lago di Como, in fact he had two villas and we'll see them both, this very week perhaps, can you imagine?"

Even Ned looked at her like she was crazed and said, "I hope there's more for our breakfast than this."

Madeleine went back out and purchased more pies and a large pot of the hot strong coffee and by noon they were finally ready. They walked behind the silent men until the coach could be reassembled and then they trundled down the far side of the mountains and through the rolling hills into the long twilight of a June evening.

Held up by rains and a broken wheel, it was nine days more until Madeleine and her brothers wandered down a cobbled path from their inn above Lago di Como to the sturdy pier, where small boats bobbed on the grey water.

"Where do we go first? asked Ned, yawning. Madeleine was older than Ned by a few minutes and he had never broken the habit of asking her opinion on all matters, which annoyed their uncle no end.

Madeleine pointed south where the lake narrowed and Ned fixed it with the owner of the boat, a talkative fellow with huge feet in ancient leather boots laced to his knees. They climbed in, the boat tipping with their weight. As the boatman rowed and raised the single square sail, Madeleine gazed at the silvery water, lit and shadowed as the sun was revealed and hidden by fast high clouds. She could swim, of course, but for how long with her heavy linen skirts in this icy water? She'd been so impatient that they come over the pass just as soon as the snows had melted away. The water hadn't yet warmed to a summertime shimmering blue-green. Instead the lake was dark, nearly black in places, and she could feel its cold breath on her wrists, above her gloves, and on the back of her neck, where her hair was coiled in a loose bun. For a moment, she felt afraid. Yet it was magical to stare at the mountains they'd just descended, their tips touched with the last glitter of ice and even the air over the lake whirling and parting, seeming fabricated of mist or clouds.

Too soon, they reached the landing pier on the far side of the lake and the boys jumped out, Ned forgetting to offer her a hand. She was embarrassed that the boatman noticed and averted his eyes. Perhaps they weren't of the quality he was used to. Uncle had warned her, when he handed her the purse and letters of credit, that the funds were not unlimited and travel, being so hugely expensive, meant that they had coin for at most four months. Four months for a tour the wealthier could extend over four years if they chose, taking their leisurely time to see all the architecture and art and learn the languages and enjoy the warm turn of the seasons from apricots to lemons to grapes for crushing into wine. And they had no tutor nor guide nor even servants accompanying them, only herself. Dwelling on inequities was pointless and Madeleine rarely wasted her time on such thoughts. But the responsibility made her irritable with her brothers when they wouldn't get out of bed and the morning was wasted, or when they requested more and more food and she had to spend their precious, limited coin.

She shook off her thoughts. She must not fritter away her time with nonsense; she was here, was she not? Nothing else mattered.

In fact, the first of the famous villas rose directly above them. She could well understand why it was named "Tragedia," situated as it was on high ground overlooking the undulating landscape and the flattened silver of the water below. She wondered who had lived here in all the years since Pliny and what it might be like to live within a family whose wealth and possessions and power extended so far. As they trudged up the uneven path, the smell of lush vegetation damp with morning dew assailed her, and she ignored the way her brothers chased each other up the path and tried instead to imagine inhabiting such a palace in the pleasurable heat of summer, wiling hot weeks away within endless gardens of lush palms and oranges growing at intervals against stone walls latticed with falls of fragrant jasmine.

They viewed the high-ceilinged chambers of the palace, so ornate, the walls covered with paintings and scrollwork and gilt, so over full her eyes tired and she crossed to the tall windows and looked out on the still grey water. Her brothers, bored, had finished with the palace. She saw them heading up the steps to the higher reaches of the garden, the two younger boys behind Ned, racing up a winding stairway lined with potted lemon trees, whooping.

When Madeleine turned to go after them, there was a woman standing in the doorway, her hand stretched out as though to stop her. She was dressed in a rather strange fashion, all in cherry red, the color in such contrast to her pale skin and dark hair and solemn expression. Madeleine started to speak, but the woman held up a hand once more and Madeleine felt the words falter on her lips. When she looked closer she realized the woman was older than she'd thought and when she blinked the woman was suddenly gone.

Madeleine frowned and went to the door and looked through. But the next chamber, with its walls of veined pink and cream marble and its immense gold-framed mirrors, was empty and quiet and she could hear no receding footsteps.

She returned to the window, still frowning, and there were her brothers shouting and joking on the terrace above the garden steps. She was glad suddenly to see their ordinary familiar play. She felt quite odd, she realized, chilly all over, her heart uneven in her chest as though she were ill. She retraced her steps, her boots clacking too loud on the marble floors and going faster and faster, until she came out once more into bright hot sun.

Outside, she felt silly. It was probably a housekeeper or maid or some such, the strange bright clothes just some custom or uniform here and nothing odd at all. She walked briskly towards her brothers, glad of their ordinary laughter when she rejoined them, and they strolled on together, past the orderly pots of lilies and nearly gone gardenias until they went down the damp stone stairs again to the waiting boat.

Six days later, having seen Pliny's second villa, the "Comedia," and several of the other famed gardens and palaces about the lake, her brothers wanted to return to the first garden they'd visited, having a plan to settle a bet about who would be the fastest sailor. They rented two boats this time, though Madeleine protested the extravagance, and then they tossed a coin to decide who had to take her along, a penance for her extra weight. Ned lost and she climbed into his boat. She felt uneasy as her brothers shouted and laughed and raised their sails in the gusty wind, though that was silly and the best way to overcome the odd dream she'd had three times this week was surely to revisit the villa and put to rest the strangeness of the woman in the cherry dress.

They reached the other shore with no mishaps and her brothers bought sausages and ale while she waited and watched them eat. She wasn't hungry and when she realized she was sticking to her brothers, almost as though she were afraid, she made herself leave them and climb the narrow shadowy streets and enter the double doors of the villa by herself. She wandered the dim rooms, their ornate chandeliers unlit, silent and empty as the other tourists were all eating luncheon by the pier. She examined the idyllic landscape paintings, with cherubs eating their dinner on scythed lawns, smooth green and lit by sunshine. She should be lecturing her brothers about the painters and their aims, she thought with a stab of guilt, but the truth was they were not interested, not even Ned.

Looking out at the lake from one of the tall windows, Madeleine noticed a wind darken the water, sweeping a trail of purple over the soft grey. A moment later, the same wind or a draft encircled her ankles and made her look round, though when she did, there was nothing, of course, to see.

Still she found herself striding down a long corridor past a row of tapestries depicting fantastical boars and crocodiles and heading out the huge oak doors encased in iron scrollwork. Ned was out there, climbing the stone stairs. "Wait," she called after him, but he didn't seem to hear her. She followed, skirts snapping in the rising wind, and then she lifted the heavy cloth above her ankles and ran after him, compelled, she wasn't sure why, to follow.

She reached the central terrace where three white peacocks lived. A male was putting on his proud display, spreading his tail feathers and shaking his feet in a strange dance. A crowd of small boys pointed at the bird and laughed, but she looked beyond the crowd, searching for Ned and couldn't find him. When she approached, the peacock fixed its eye on her and furled its tail feathers in a menacing way, then rounded on one of the boys with its unearthly scream. The boys yelled and scattered and Madeleine was left alone in the hot sun, with only an odd sweet odor of some strange flower that seemed to invade the air.

Later that day, Madeleine sat on a granite step and looked out over the light and shadow of the garden, at the pots of pansies flowering madly and the peacock strutting and the waving fronds of an enormous willow tree. She considered again her repeated dream, let herself entertain the mad idea that the woman in the cherry dress was some inhabitant from another time. Was it possible that she'd not been real, not a servant or strange foreigner, was it possible that the woman had, in other words, been a ghost? An ancient garden like this must surely be haunted, if such a thing were possible. Indeed, all of Italy might be full of such ghosts. But she didn't believe in ghosts, though she was certainly interested in the past. She believed in history and memory, and in learning, whether art or numbers. What would a ghost want with her anyway? What message could a ghost possibly have for her? She was just a visitor, passing through, one among so very many.

The sun emerged from a pile of puffy clouds and warmed her knees through the fabric of her dark skirt. She was drowsy, she's stayed up so late last night, filling in her brothers' trip record with sketches of towers and garden paths and rare birds, all neatly labeled in her careful script. And then waking with that strange dream, a feeling of uneasy chill lingering into the day.

She leaned her head back against the granite wall and closed her eyes, smelling the beguiling mix of warm moss and ferns. Perhaps she dozed. She felt a cool hand touch the back of her neck and slide a finger down her arm; cool fingers encircled her wrist. She blinked, and sat up straight. The sun had backed behind a swathe of dark purple clouds and as she shook herself awake a fork of lightning split the sky and she heard the rush of wind that signaled rain.

She stumbled to her feet. Where were her brothers?

She descended the steps, wind blowing her skirts to tangle about her ankles. A door banged in the distance. They would have to hurry; it might be dangerous out on the lake. And surely it was late, much later than she'd thought. It was nearly dark under the cedars as she ran. A second slash of lightening and sharp crack of thunder. They would have to wait it out. She descended the mossy steps, but when she reached the boat landing, it was quite deserted. The boats were gone, her brothers weren't at the tables, and indeed the restaurant looked closed, its windows shuttered tight. Madeleine rushed back into the street, rain coming down suddenly, soaking her gown and hair in an instant. The street was also deserted, the shops shut tight and only a sodden cat glaring at her from behind a rusted pail.

"Where have you been?" said Ned, grabbing her elbow. "Come on, the boat is waiting."

"We can't go onto the lake now," Madeleine said, but he just shook his head and ignored her. She gathered up her skirts and ran after him, slipping on the wet cobbles with her old boots.

Rob and Sam waited under a drenched canvas umbrella, their hands clutching the ropes holding the boats to the loose boards forming a makeshift pier. "We have to wait out the storm," Madeleine repeated, but Ned untied his boat and gestured to her impatiently to climb in. "Are you sure?" asked Madeleine, but the younger boys cast off their boats and so she clambered in and sat by the mast on the wooden stool, driving rain soaking her skirts so they clung to her knees.

As they left the tiny bay, the gusts of wind picked up and Madeleine clutched her arms around her chest and stared at the grey water, wind sheeting across in dark triangles. Her brothers were excited, exhilarated by the storm, laughing and shouting taunts at each other. But she couldn't help thinking about their parents. The younger boys had hardly known them, of course, but Ned should recall. She glanced at him, but he was tugging at the line holding up the sail at half-mast. The rain had plastered his dark hair, so like hers, to his neck and his grey eyes looked away from her, out over the water. He looked just as she looked when she peered at herself in the mirror in the morning and yet somehow he looked like a stranger, for the first time.

Madeleine clutched her arms tighter to her chest, uneasy at the mere thought. Her parents had drowned, their carriage toppling from a bridge in midwinter, falling twenty feet into black icy water. She never dreamt about that, but it was a clear picture in her mind, always lurking and easily recalled, the gilt-painted carriage under the black water, the doors tightly shut, the wood swollen so no one could open them, the windows small and tiny and curtained, the lace waving gently in the currents, obscuring the faces inside.

There was a shout from Rob.

"Pull in the sail, you've too much sail out," shouted Ned.

"I'm going to win," shouted Rob, waving one arm while holding the line with the other.

"Fool," muttered Ned.

Then a gust billowed out their sail and snapped the boom across. "Duck Maddy," yelled Ned. That he used her childhood name frightened her. She found herself crouched on the floor of the boat, water sloshing around her boots. Her ankles burned with the cold. Ned got the boat righted and lowered the sail rapidly into an uneven pile. The smell of wet wool and lake water filled her nostrils.

She looked out for Sam and Rob. Sam had just reached the shore. She saw him leap from the boat and wave, a tiny figure in the shifting fog. But Rob she couldn't see at all.

"Ned?"

Ned looked up from the sail he was folding away and cursed under his breath. His hands, she noticed, were red with cold and his nose was running. His eyes, stronger than hers, searched the lake and she watched his face and felt a small cold stone form in the center of her chest. "Rob," she called out, jumping to her feet.

"Sit down," yelled Ned, throwing his weight on her shoulders and forcing her down onto the wet sail. "You'll sink us for certain."

"Where is he?" she asked in a small voice.

Ned shook his head and took up the oars and rowed, saying nothing, until the boat ground on the rocks on the shore and Sam was helping haul her up the beach. "He went over," she heard him whisper to Ned. "He went over and just never came up."

Four weeks passed, excruciating weeks, the lake shrouded in clouds. Finally, the sun returned and with it the heat that finally promised high summer. It was noon and Madeleine sat in the garden of the inn near the lake where they'd taken two rooms while the authorities searched for Rob and they waited, for news or for whatever would come. Her fingers pleated and re-pleated the cloth in her skirt. Around her, the garden steamed in the humidity and the heart shaped palm leaves seemed to quiver and hum.

"Maddy, where are you? Why are you just sitting there?" Ned strode into the garden, brushing past the giant bougainvillea vine, which spattered water in dark drops across his linen shirt, open at the neck.

"I'm trying to think what else we should do," said Madeleine.

Ned dropped down onto the chair beside her and shrugged. "Nothing, we have done what we can."

The young serving girl from the restaurant below the inn entered the garden. Madeleine leaped up. "Have you news?"

The servant shook her head. "Only a letter." She ignored Madeleine's outstretched hand and gave Ned the sealed missive.

Ned ripped it apart, pulled out a long note, and handed it to Madeleine. He could barely read. He said the letters danced across the page and she'd always done his reading for him.

She recognized the slashing cursive already. "It's from Uncle."

Ned cursed under his breath.

She scanned the page. "He's telling us to come home immediately and have the body sent on. He's arranged the funds."

"Has he," said Ned in a harsh voice. "And has he arranged for us to find the body too?"

"Ned, don't be that way," said Madeleine. Her fingers, holding the letter, were shaking. She read on, but it was all about the logistics for their return.

She placed the letter on the rickety iron table between them and twined her hands together behind her back. The end of her Tour. She would never get another chance. That she could even think such a dreadfully selfish thought made her wince. She couldn't meet Ned's eyes.

"I meant to tell you sooner, or in a better way at least," said Ned.

"Tell me what?"

Ned was examining the far side of the garden, where tall cypresses shut out the light. "I'm not going back with you. I'm not going home. That is, I've taken a position here."

"Here?" said Madeleine, looking around the quiet garden, then at her twin. "What can you mean?"

"Well, you're always saying how fine it is here in Italy, and it is fine. I'm on my own here and I quite like it. I've taken a position as a gardener. On an estate outside Verona."

"You're going to be a gardener?" said Madeleine. Her mind felt slow and stupid. "Is this because I wouldn't let you handle the money?" Two weeks back Ned had walked into her chamber and demanded she let him take over the handling of the funds. She hadn't let him of course; Uncle had been quite clear that though she was a woman, Ned could hardly be trusted with keeping track of their expenses.

"Yes. A gardener. I've been promised head gardener in time. It's not like I can do much else. I'll never be a law clerk or do accounts. You're the one with the mind Maddy, you know that. You should be the man." He frowned and tugged at his collar. "And I'm not gentlemen, not really, we haven't the income, you know that too. Uncle's been kind, but I'm not a child any longer. I have to do something with my life."

"But Ned, how will you live here, all alone? What will I do without you, I never thought…" Her voice trailed off.

"We're grown now, Maddy. It's all going to be different." He patted her arm awkwardly. "And I'm glad of it, for one. You'll need to take Sam home, of course."

He strode out of the garden and Madeleine stared after him, at the hole in the cypress wall that served as a doorway, an entrance or an exit, obscuring whatever lay on the other side.

True to his word, and despite her most persuasive arguments and even unusual tears, Ned left just two days later, carrying one trunk, taking one-third of their coin, and hugging her roughly before he walked away. Madeleine watched him go and waved when he turned. But he only waved once and tromped on and over the hill and out of her sight.

She sat on in the damp garden under a grey sky, watching lazy bees buzz around the sagging lilies, weighed down by water. She couldn't think what she needed to do next, she couldn't think really at all. They had been four and now it was just her and Sam, and perhaps Rob's body, if it could be found.

The serving girl startled her, speaking from behind her back, so that she dropped the china cup in her hand and it shattered on the slates. The girl sighed and picked up the shards. "You'd best come Miss, there's someone wanting you at the reception."

"Yes," said Madeleine, gathering her shawl and hat. "But wait, tell me," she said, "I suppose you know all the local history here?"

"I suppose," said the girl, "if you mean stories and such, about the past."

"Yes, stories. Though some are true, are they not?"

The girl shrugged. "Some are, and some aren't. But we don't know which is which."

"Has there ever been a ghost talked about, across the lake in the villa?"

The girl looked uncomfortable. "Some say so. She's called the lady who walks. She wears a red dress. Have you seen her, Miss?" The girl was whispering now, as though the lady might hear her, even across the water. "My grandmother used to speak of it. But no one talks of it now. Will you come now, they're waiting on you."

Madeleine nodded and followed the girl out of the garden. The girl's feet were bare and calloused, but her back was straight and her hair, falling out from the back of her starched cap, such as all the girls wore here, was dark and waving and lustrous with healthy life. Madeleine felt ancient and exhausted, just looking at her.

In the dim reception room, crowded with more palms and ferns in giant pots, a police officer waited, tapping with a pen on a small green book in which he was writing down some notes with laborious care. "Are you the sister?" he asked with no polite address.

Madeleine nodded. "You have found him then." Her voice wavered.

"That we have Miss, though not quite as expected."

Madeleine wondered what could have been expected and found she had few ideas, only a gruesome image of poor Rob, white and floating among weeds in some forgotten marsh. "What do you mean?"

"Where is your brother, the other one?" asked the officer.

"In the café breakfasting I think."

"Let's fetch him, shall we?" It didn't really sound like a question so Madeleine spoke to the serving girl, who raced down to the cafe, excited by the disruption of a routine morning. She waited, her fingers twined and her face composed. But she was puzzled and confused and sad, so sad it seemed that the weight of her failure would crush her down for the entire rest of her life. How had everything gone so very wrong? She had wanted so desperately to come to Italy, she had convinced her brothers, and Uncle. Without her, they would never have been here at all. She had only wanted this one small time, this few months before accepting all the rest. The required marriage to someone with coin, or failing that, nursing uncle as he grew old. As she grew old and unloved and shut out from the whole world she wished to inhabit.

A stray wind brushed across her wrists, fluttering the lace. She started and pulled down the cuffs on her sleeve. Was it all her fault? Had she killed small Rob? Insisting on this Tour, pushing for it relentlessly. Was she responsible for it all, even for Ned leaving? And she was angry too, so angry at Ned, who had walked away to his new life as though he could simply drop his burdens, his entire past, as though he could just drop her. They were supposed to be together, two parts of one whole, always. Did he hate her for what she'd done, was that it? She watched a fly buzzing around a crescent cookie, dusted with powdery sugar, which someone had left by their coffee on the table. He'd left her, his very own twin, whistling, as though leaving were a joy.

When the serving girl returned with Sam, her brother was not alone. Another boy, of similar height, with a blue cap, moving slowly on a pair of crutches, was with him. Madeleine blinked and stared, her eyes suddenly burning.

"Rob!" She rushed to him, hugging him so hard she knocked off his cap and tumbled one crutch to the slate floor with a tremendous clatter. His head was shaved bare, and a red scar with terrible white stitches wound across his scalp.

"You're not drowned," she exclaimed and went to pick him up and spin him round as she used to do, but thought better of it. She dropped her arms and smiled so wide it hurt her stiff cheeks. "How very glad I am to see you," she whispered.

"I'm glad too," Rob said, and looked the other way.

"Hey," said Sam. "I'm here as well and I was never so dumb as to fall from my boat." The boys began to argue and Madeleine sat down in a heap on the nearest velvet stool and found she was silently crying, tears rushing down her cheeks. The boys ignored her and the officers shuffled and the older man behind the counter murmured, "Shock. To be expected." Someone handed her a glass and she drank. Whatever it was burned down her throat and made her face flush with sudden warmth, welcome as summer's heat.

That night, alone in her room, with its white bedspread pulled up tight and unwrinkled and its painting of a bowl of dark cherries falling out over a polished table and its single tall dark window looking out, if she could only see it, at the lake, all Madeleine could think was that Ned didn't know and wouldn't know, wouldn't ever, unless she wrote to him, telling him the whole story, one he couldn't even read for himself. She pulled out her sketchbook, but she did not write. Instead she drew, the lake, the wilderness of trees, the red flutter of a woman's skirt as she escaped behind a wall.

THE SECRET GARDEN

Cornwall, 1966

When Ellie decided to make a garden, she knew immediately that it must be kept a secret. Henry would not approve, if he were home to disapprove, but since he wasn't, she could move ahead, though cautiously. He had the habit of appearing, pouncing was how she thought of it, with excuses like, thought you'd like me to come home for lunch, or, I forgot the ledger, or, when he was in a worse mood, you forgot to pack my papers. She had married him in London, ages ago in a kind of teenage dream, and too quickly realized she'd made a slight mistake, but there was nothing to be done about that. She was thirty-five now and he was nearly forty, and all around them the world had gone somewhat mad, launching into a psychedelic dream, full of color. But they were on the wrong side of it all.

If Henry didn't come home to disapprove, his elder sister might. Lydia was tall and straight-backed and at first Ellie imagined they'd become friends. In the posh restaurant with a ceiling of glass and a wall that was a vertical garden of fuzzy moss and granite speckled with lichen, Lydia had leaned in close, so close Ellie had caught the smell, rather musky, of her long blonde hair. She'd whispered something, which Ellie hadn't quite caught and then gone off, shaking her hair down her back like a rippling mane. The only word she'd really heard was somnolent, but that could hardly be right, and since then Lydia had kept her distance.

Ellie edged out the back door of their two story townhouse, into the pale sun. Tree branches from two large oaks stretched over the yard, dappling it with unwanted shade. She held a hand to her forehead to cut the glare and examined them. If she cut three or four limbs, she thought the shade would be sufficiently diminished and if she did it one branch this week and one the next, she thought Henry would never notice. It wasn't often that he paid attention to the yard, and when he did it was to quickly mow the grass and yank out weeds all the while complaining that she should have done the yard work herself, for after all, what did she really do all day with her time.

Ellie let him talk to her that way because she knew what he truly meant; she knew his heart ached sometimes, when he let it, even as much as hers. They'd tried, of course, but it was as though no child could be commenced here, in this sterile suburban street where every house had the same mailbox and blue morning-glory vine and brick path leading the way to the front door. But that couldn't be true because after dinner the street rang with the shouts of children playing kick ball in the dusk.

Ellie dug for most of that first afternoon, and afterwards, washing her hands over and over in the sink, she decided she'd best buy gardening gloves to hide the nicks and dirt stained into her palms and creeping under her fingernails. And that little decision was the beginning of the deception.

Deceiving, she found, is actually quite hard work. It took weeks and then months for Ellie to learn the ins and outs of it. The first task was to cut the tree branches and hide the pale ovals of shocked open wood and she accomplished this, partly by holding a party right there in the open of the yard.

"It looks so nice out here," said her friend Nicole, looking around with a puzzled frown marring her perfectly drawn black eyebrows. Nicole was a model in clothing catalogs and was generally as good looking in person as in her photos, which is not, Ellie knew, always the case. Next to her Ellie always felt too white, too plump, her maxi linen skirt too wrinkled and her breasts a touch too low and slightly sagging. Before Henry could look around and wonder what Nicole meant, Ellie put a finger on his wrist and asked him to start the grill and then he was occupied with making lamb burgers topped with feta and grilled zucchini and never got back to asking. Nicole collapsed on a chaise and stroked the stripe of sunlight on her bared thigh while she sipped her diet coke. She never ate at these neighborhood gatherings or perhaps at all. The models in the glossy magazines were all like that, tiny, bird-boned, so so skinny in their short short skirts. Ellie thought a moment, then sent the teenage daughter of the librarian who lived across the street over to ask Nicole about becoming a model and that distracted Nicole, who loved to talk about her career. The danger passed and the party went on well into the dark, sparkling with the twinkling café lights she'd draped around the patio, and everyone seemed to drink a lot of sweet red wine and in their farewells deemed the party a great success.

And so it went, week by week. After a month, sunlight flooded the yard at noon and in the morning there were quiet grey spaces filled with shifting fog and in the evening the orange sun glowed right over the end of the yard and Ellie spent her nights, lying awake beside a sleeping Henry, imagining what special and significant object she could put there, in that orange comforting light, something to create a kind of magic that would stir the garden to life.

Ellie read books too, checking them out of the public library two towns over with a falsified library card to avoid her neighbor who worked in the library just down the road. Who would have imagined she'd known how to create a false ID? But it seemed that knowledge had been there all along, waiting until needed, in a corner of her mind. She wondered what other untapped resources she contained.

The books were full of theories. A garden must reveal and conceal. A garden is a narrative. Every garden is a commentary on the Garden of Eden or Paradise or both. And so forth. She read these articles, dutifully, sometimes making notes in pencil on an index card, but it was the photographs that held her attention. Leaves, blossoms, stems, pathways, horizontal and vertical accents, focal points.

In that first autumn, she dug three long narrow borders and covered them with maple and oak leaves so they were hidden and looked exactly like the rest of the backyard. Henry had taken to staying out later and later, working into the evening, and even when he did get home and she set his reheated dinner plate in front of him, the broccoli pale and wilted, he read his newspaper while he shoved it in and barely spoke with her at all. One evening she noticed his hair was certainly thinner at the top and she stayed awake a very long time that night feeling guilt so heavy it seemed to sit on her stomach and pin her to the bed.

The next morning, she suggested they go away together, to the seaside, for a vacation. Henry stared at her over his paper, egg dripping from his fork and suddenly he smiled, just like he used to smile and said, "Let's do that, but it can't be this weekend."

"Next?" she said, already regretting the impulse.

"No," he said, "Let's go now, not this weekend, right now, today."

The man with the mulch was coming today. But she couldn't put Henry off without alerting him and soon they were throwing a few clothes and swim suits into a bag and Henry was actually whistling as he carried it down the stairs and they were in the car driving away. She had called the mulch guy while Henry backed the car out from the garage and left a message and hoped for the best.

They arrived at the beach town, somewhere outside the busyness of Bath, about four pm.

"Now what?" Henry said, his air of decision seeming to deflate all at once, as they faced the row of faded beach houses, each painted a different shade of blue. The sea stretched out from the pebble beach, silver and pale violet in the late afternoon light. They could smell salt and something muskier and more enticing, like bait.

"Looking for a place to stay?" A middle-aged couple, slightly older, stood before them, the husband jovial, his nose burnt red and peeling, the wife holding his arm and wearing a damp sundress over a bikini.

"We are rather," said Ellie, when Henry didn't answer.

"We have a great one, and the landlady throws in a good breakfast, eggs and tomatoes and beans, French toast even, to go with the fry up," said the husband.

"Served on a delightful porch overlooking her garden," said the wife. "Do come along, I know she's got a few rooms left. It's rather late, isn't it, for the real season."

So they trailed after the damp and sandy couple and Ellie wondered what the temperature of the sea was and if she should wear her sneakers or sandals when they strolled out to the beach after dinner. Mostly she thought about the garden of the landlady. She hoped it would be a proper English garden, nothing formal, more a restless bed of riotous dahlias and asters and ungainly clumps of broom grass.

The landlady was thin and dressed in ironed running clothes. She efficiently settled them into a corner room in the back. "Quiet," she said, "and you've got your own bath and all here. Breakfast seven to nine sharp. Tea outside your door at 6. I don't abide all that late rising stuff." She whizzed out the door. The wind caught the door and slammed it shut after her, so that it seemed like she was angry with them, though Ellie was pretty sure she was not.

The room was quiet, as promised, and busy with brown flowered wallpaper and coral shades on the glass lamps, and the bed a little too soft, but it would all do. "Well," Ellie said, "dinner?"

Henry was pulling out his yellow legal pad. "Oh," he said awkwardly, "yes, I guess that's right," and he wedged it behind the lamp on the bedside table and tucked in his shirt.

Out on the lawn, a sprinkler was running and waddling around in the spray of water was a mother mallard and a string of chicks, barely more than brown balls of fluff. The water didn't seem to deter them or soak their fluff at all. They were perfectly at home and marched back and forth after their mother in a line. One chick trailed behind.

"Gull will get that one," said Henry.

"Don't say it," said Ellie, but she knew he was right, it would happen, sooner or later. Ducks couldn't be unusual, they had to fall in line.

They ate chicken for dinner, though duck was also on the menu. The chicken was stewed in apricots in a kind of Persian-style dish, explained the teenage waitress in a breathless voice. That was a new thing for both of them and they picked at the food before deciding it was okay.

After dinner they did go for that stroll. Arm in arm, because it seemed the thing to do, they walked down the crescent of beach to the far end where a sea wall stretched out. "Shall we keep going?" said Ellie.

The setting sun was lighting up the water with a glow and she really meant, let's go back. She wanted to climb into bed and think about home and plan her garden. She was homesick, being here in this strange place and even her husband seemed like a stranger to her here and now.

"What's that?" said Henry.

They gazed out in the gleaming water and both gasped at the same time, thinking it was a child. But then what seemed a pale arm turned into a leg. "It's a dog," said Henry, starting forward.

"But," said Ellie, "don't, it's just a dog."

Henry had his shirt off already. "It's not going to make it," he said.

Ellie looked out at the bright water and the thrashing, small and silent, in the middle. "No," she said.

But Henry was already gone, running down the beach. He splashed and then dove into the water and was already swimming out. Ellie ran down too, into the waves, calf deep. The water was icy and gripped her ankles and the waves sucked sand out from under her heels and toes. She stumbled once and backed out. Henry was swimming freestyle and the wind carried away the splash of his arms and legs. She was watching a kind of silent movie where the brave hero saves the heroine's pet. Only it wasn't her pet and she didn't care about the dog at all. She watched Henry and wondered what he was thinking. Did he care about the dog? Was he trying to impress her? Was he just trying to do something, anything? She glanced away, hearing the rumble of a tractor or truck behind her.

"Fool," said a deep voice. "He won't get there in time."

It was the lifeguard with his truck and white floating rings emblazoned with red. "What's your dog's name?"

"It's not our dog," said Ellie faintly.

The lifeguard sighed, the blonde hair on his wide chest wiggling. Ellie swallowed and looked away. He shoved the inflatable raft with its giant engine off the tractor and into the water, climbed in, revved up the engine and was off over the surf and into the flattened swells beyond, leaving a wake behind.

"You don't even like dogs," said Ellie a week later, as she cleared the plates after dinner, pork chops and mashed potatoes and steamed carrots. She could hear how cross she sounded.

Henry shrugged and took a bite of hot roll. "I had a collie when I was a boy."

She thought about the collie, picturing it lolling at her much younger husband's feet. "No really, why did you do it?"

Henry hesitated, then ate his last mouthful. "I've got to go out," he said.

Ellie nodded. He went out every night now, just about. She tried to prevent herself from wondering where he went and why.

When he was gone, she lugged out her garden notebook and sat down on the lilac couch in the living room with the notebook open on her lap. It had grown thick and heavy, crammed with all her sketches and possible designs. She leafed through her stack of nursery catalogs, with pages marked and selections circled. She filled in the order forms in ink, ordering all the plants she needed. They would arrive in the spring, the back of the catalog announced to her in exuberant capitals, ready for planting. Be sure to be ready to put them in the ground right away. She was a little shocked at the end price, 462 pounds, but then she shrugged. The bank account could take it, and she did all the bills anyway.

The winter months dragged by, bleak with slush and darkness, and Ellie put the garden out of her mind. She took a night class on botanical watercolors to fill up those empty evenings. They never made love now, so it wasn't likely a child would come to liven things up; it was all up to them and they didn't seem to be up to the challenge. It seemed to take so much energy, being a couple. She watched the neighbors at the Christmas parties, marching in and out and drinking eggnog with efficiency and determination. She watched old movies, black and white, never in color. She watched the snowflakes fall one evening, so fat and heavy and white in the blue-black silent dark.

Henry did whatever it was he was doing. There was no clue on the credit card. He either was using cash, or he'd opened a new card, or he really was going to work every night.

It was a longer than normal winter. A long winter and a cold rainy spring. But one morning in late April the bell rang and when Ellie came to the door, the postman was already lugging in boxes and piling them on her porch. So many boxes. Had she really ordered all of that? She tumbled them into the house so the neighbors wouldn't see, and stood with her eyes shut and breath coming fast, boxes stacked around her in the hall.

Then she climbed the stairs and got out her plans, stored all winter under their mattress, and pulled on her gloves and got to work. It took her all morning just to rip open the boxes and pull out the plants, some just roots wrapped in wet newspaper and others trailing tiny fragile leaves. Around noon, a weak sun came out, and she put her plan onto the wet grass, held down by rocks on each corner, and dug in the cold earth. She worked until late in the afternoon, and when she was finally done, her shoulders ached but the garden was completely planted. She rolled up her damp plans and shoved them in the trash can in the shed and went indoors, warm stale air hitting her cold cheeks.

She took off her boots and coat and padded into the living room and stared out the window into the near dark. The garden didn't look anything like she'd imagined. Nothing like the pictures in the catalog. The plants were tiny and looked like they'd struggle to just stay alive and the hedge meant to hide the secret garden from the ordinary patio was only knee high and full of gaps.

Ellie showered and made an unusual evening cup of coffee and drank it in three scalding gulps looking out the window at the exposed bed with its fragile inhabitants. Then she went back upstairs and pulled out a new dress from the back of her closet, one with a flowing pattern of leaves and flowers, a low square neck, and an extravagant ruffle at the floor length hem, of the sort she wanted to wear but never had the chance. She put a bottle of chablis to chill in the fridge.

Once, back in the months when they first married, in bed after they'd made love, Henry had described a garden to her, one he'd played in as a child on a family trip to the country, the garden of some long dead great aunt. But he'd talked about it using extravagant words, words like glowing and exuberant and amber and glorious, poetical words he never had used with her before. Even his voice had been different, low and compelling and urgent. He'd never spoken like that again. She'd wondered over the months and years if it had been because he regretted the impulse, or if she hadn't responded correctly somehow. She regretted the catch in her throat that made it so hard to just ask.

She smoothed her dress down over her hips and went downstairs. She made a green salad and simmered chicken in mustard and cream. She dragged the table from the dining room into the living room and over to the bay window. She set the table with new green placemats and white plates and filled two water glasses, the ice chiming gently when she walked back to the kitchen and got the matches. She lit the candles, filled the wine glasses, and waited. Henry was late, but he would come.

Standing at the living room window, she gazed out into the black night, seeing darkness and her own reflection, distorted and glamorous, in the glass. She turned on the backyard switch she'd had installed, which lit the garden with a looping string of café lights. She thought they looked magical and serene and made the garden somewhere out of time.

Would he recognize his garden from her efforts? Would he understand what she meant to say, though she had no words to reach across their silence? Would the language of whispering plants speak to him somehow?

She heard a step at the front door and she rushed over and opened it wide, before he could touch the handle.

His eyes met hers, surprised.

"I have something for you," she said.

THE SMALLEST BIRDS

Small birds, like hummingbirds but larger, beat their wings and darted in so close that Sophie flinched. The tiny café, situated amongst pots of marguerites, overlooking the shimmering lake, had seemed so peaceful. She'd selected a seat under a palm with wide fringes for leaves, under a table dappled with shifting light and shadow, and studied the short menu with anticipation. After ordering apricot cake and a double espresso, she'd pulled out her novel, but when the cake arrived, so did the insistent birds, drawn irresistibly to the crumbs and some scent only they could find in the air. She tried to shoo them away, but they were intractable, and she felt how ineffective she was.

They drove her away. She gulped her espresso and paid her eight euros, which would have been a reasonable price, had she sat there for an hour or even two as she'd planned, but now she had read only two pages and it was too early for the ferry back to the mainland. She was on Isola Madre in the middle of Lago di Maggiore in the north of Italy, and since she'd arrived on the first boat this morning, she'd already seen the island's gardens and three fountains and even the still pool coated with water lilies and buzzing with strange large bees and there was nothing really left to do.

She scuffed along the gravel path overlooking the lake. Along the path, a line of blossoming trees in huge terracotta pots formed a fragrant hedge so there was just her, the scent of lemons mixed with lake water, and the silvery green water stretching off to a bird's egg sky. Ridiculously, she found herself fighting back tears. And she was the one who'd wanted to be here, who'd planned and saved, spending her lunch hour and plenty of her work time too, studying the photo gallery on the website advertising the independent tour to the famous gardens of the Italian Lakes. "Perfect for the adventurous solo traveler!" So what was she crying about? The promised Italian sun was indeed shining down and it was not a hardship, surely, to linger here walking another hour or two.

A middle-aged couple ambled in front of her, pointing to leaves and discussing, Sophie assumed, the merits of the different plants. She heard some Latin names mumbled. They were speaking English with a British accent and nodding politely to each person who passed. They seemed so content with each other's presence, so amiable to each other, so completely the opposite of how it had been with her and Martin lately, and even at the start.

She fiddled with the cell phone in her skirt pocket. Perhaps there was reception here? Wandering over to a bench in front of several cypress trees, she sat and watched a lizard slither off the path into some fallen leaves. She checked around her feet, clad in sensible sandals and knee socks, to make sure no other creatures lingered amidst the broken cones. She took the phone out and laid it in her lap.

Across a meadow dotted with buttercups, the lake tossed choppy waves in a newly risen breeze, almost green as a sea. And beyond the lake, the mountains of Switzerland looked just as majestic as Alps should look. Everything was exactly as the brochure had promised. Sophie pressed Martin's name on her contact list. She'd demoted him from number one a fortnight ago, but she hadn't been able to quite wipe him off her list, some glitch making his name reappear again and again. The phone rang twice, three times, but he never picked up until four. She hung up and got to her feet. The phone vibrated in her hand. "Hello?" she said softly.

"Why are you calling me Sophie?"

His voice was so familiar and his tone so abrupt.

"I'm at work, in a meeting. I thought you said we were not going to do this."

She hesitated. "I just thought I'd see how you were doing?"

"How I'm doing? What do you care about that? I'm in a meeting, Sophie. I know that means nothing to you. Oh forget it."

There was a decisive click as he hung up.

The middle-aged couple passed her, returning from their walk along the orange bower, the woman carrying a flowering bud of some exotic white plant in her hand. A large dark bird, maybe a hawk, flew overhead, and a cloud should have blotted out the sun but didn't. Instead brilliant sun beat down on her head, which ached, right behind her eyes, as though just seeing all this immense and symmetrical beauty was painful.

A week later, Sophie perched on the edge of the bed in her three-star hotel room in Milan. She could hear cars beeping and the boom of the bass from the rock concert going on in the square in front of the ornate cathedral. Every night there was noise. Last night it had been a mass, complete with a bishop or maybe a cardinal, in a bright red robe. The teenagers milling around hadn't appeared to be listening. They slouched against each other, smoking cigarettes, laughing, but some of those rants must be insinuating themselves into their malleable brains.

How young and malleable her own brain had been, when she'd first met Martin. He'd been older seeming, smoking his own cigarette, holding it in that European way between finger and thumb. She'd been awkward, badly dressed, and yearning for adventure her junior year abroad. It was Paris after all. It had seemed a kind of miracle, bound up with the whole idea of Europe and so magical as to be entirely out of her control. And after that, they'd been together for nineteen years. Nearly half of her life. Could that even be possible? Yet now here she was, washed up on the shore of this bland Milanese hotel, doing another free-lance journalism job, while on vacation from her real job at the travel agency. The design show at the Navigli, the subject of her article, had been glittering and immense and intimidating and she'd abandoned it after one afternoon, but the article was due in less than a week. She went to the plate glass window and peered out into the blue dusk. Lights twinkled and merged with unseeable stars in the darkening sky.

She must do something, she decided, right now. To sit here one more night was unbearable. The AC in the room emitted a musty smell and she felt like her head was full of its mildew.

She grabbed her phone from the night table and her black notebook and slipped out of her sandals. She rummaged in her suitcase and pulled out the high heels she'd bought on Tuesday, shopping in the high-ceilinged mall at Milan's center. The shoes were spring green silk, with patent leather heels and a zigzag line of silver, looking rather like lightning, running along the outside edge by her little toe. She put them on and tried walking, back and forth. She could just do it. She grabbed up a purple shawl and her purse and went out the door, letting it slam shut behind her in the echoing corridor.

Descending in the elevator, she examined her reflection in the full-length mirror. Her feet looked wild and sexy and her eyes looked afraid and there were tiny wrinkles fanning out from the left corner of her mouth. What else could one expect at nearly forty? She fluffed up her hair and looked away from the several strands of grey that mingled with the brown.

She clicked out of the hotel, as though she knew how to walk in heels, hoping not to slip on the marble floor. She knew enough to watch out for water. It was a warm enveloping night, the air silky against her bare arms. There was a smell of cheap perfumes and popcorn and some spice in the air, or maybe it was coffee. She turned left and walked, not meeting the eye of any of the wanderers drifting at the edge of the crowd. The band was taking a break and people were strolling and eating cotton candy and drinking red wine straight from the bottle.

She pulled out her phone and examined herself in the gleaming black glass of a storefront window. She pointed the phone at her reflection and managed to include her shoes. Good, it was good. She posted the picture off to Martin. Then she turned off the phone and struck off down a narrow street lined with bars and cafes, people spilling onto the street, car horns blaring. She took another street, even more narrow, and another until she was in an unfamiliar area. There were fewer people here, and they were mostly men, and they stared when she walked by. She put on her sunglasses, though it was nearly full dark, and ignored them.

She approached a piazza lined with cypress trees in huge pots. A burst of laughter came from a café in the far corner. She crossed the pavement, stepping over the hoses for watering the trees, and sat down at a tiny table with one chair, under a wide yellow umbrella. No one else was sitting outside. Indoors, a noisy crowd of young men watched some sports event, probably soccer, or football as they called it here. She took off her sunglasses and examined her feet. She was getting a tiny blister on her left heel, but it was worth it. She'd go shopping again tomorrow, she decided, and get more heels. Perhaps those cherry red ones with the twining ankle straps. She liked heels, though she'd never worn them as they made her even taller, and Martin had been just her height. It would be a decisive move, and Italy was certainly the place to get shoes. But was it a move in the right direction? Suddenly she wanted to call someone, just to talk it over, all of it, but she never did that. And who, after all, would she call? Martin was the one she talked to.

She picked up the heavy silver fork and flipped it round and round in her fingers. How solitary she had become. How lonely. When had that happened? She took out her phone and held it until it warmed in her palm. Then she placed it on her napkin beside the knife.

The waiter came out finally and she ordered a half carafe of Montepulciano and some olives with lemon slices. When the wine came she sipped it and ate two olives and stared across the piazza, watching the pigeons coo and chase each other, her legs crossed, one shoe dangling.

"Perhaps we can join you," said a voice.

Sophie looked up. A man and a woman, the woman wearing black flats and a blue hat shoved down over straight auburn hair. The man was fiftyish and fit, with grey-hair and European-style rectangular glasses.

"Thank you," said the woman, not waiting for an answer and pulling over a chair. The man dragged over another and they sat down opposite her and waited.

"Would you like some wine?" asked Sophie, when they said nothing. Somehow she seemed to be the hostess in this odd gathering.

"Lovely," said the woman, taking off her hat and creasing it as she folded it into four quarters and stuffed it in her raincoat pocket. "Please order for us, we'd have no idea."

Perhaps they were tourists and they thought she was Italian? Sophie gestured to the waiter, who sent a longing glance at the TV screen but sprinted over and took her order for a full carafe of the house red and some pecorino and bread. She was glad she had studied her conversational Italian so diligently all winter.

The order completed, the waiter left, switching on the café lights as he went back inside. The tiny lights twinkled in draped scallops, enclosing them as though in a tent. The husband took off and polished his glasses. His wife, Sophie assumed it was his wife, ruffled through her purse and came up with antiseptic hand wipes. "You can't be too careful," she said. "We're from Devon. Where is your home?"

Sophie hesitated. She couldn't say Boston at this point. They'd be embarrassed if they'd really thought she was Italian. "Rome," she said.

"How marvelous," said the woman, with a wide smile. She began to speak of Rome, how she'd always wanted to go there, and how she'd studied the history, all twenty-six centuries of it, at school. She described the building techniques of the masons making the city walls in some detail and Sophie found herself surprisingly entertained. Now that they were talking, the couple chattered on, or rather the woman chattered on, her husband contently drinking the wine and watching the pigeons pick at crumbs. Loud cheers from indoors erupted every so often and they'd all look over and wait and then go on. Eventually the woman said something about the lake.

"What lake," interrupted Sophie, who had drunk three glasses of wine now, she estimated, though it was hard to tell when you kept topping up your glass.

"Maggiore of course. Well, that's where we know you from," said the woman, staring, as though she'd said something quite odd.

Sophie frowned. It couldn't be, but apparently it was, the amiable gardening middle-aged couple from Isola Madre. How long ago that already seemed. But they were right, what was wrong with her? Why hadn't she recognized them? And why had they noticed her? Suddenly, she felt embarrassed, caught sitting alone. Her fingers itched to pick up her phone and see if Martin had responded to her selfie. It sat on her napkin, reflecting the twinkling lights, gleaming and tempting her. "I had to leave," she said to the couple. "I was the one who had to go. I had to come on this trip, just get straight away." She closed her lips so the sound inside her, something urgent, could not get out.

The woman's brows drew together and she looked at her husband, who stared down at the table, his finger tracing a circle in the puddle of water from the wine glass.

"Martin and I," continued Sophie, "we seemed to belong together. Everyone said so, and we've been happy I think. As much as anyone can be, being alive I mean."

The wife stared at her, her eyes alarmed now. "Well, I don't know," she began.

"I do know," said Sophie. She took another gulp of wine. "How can I go on as before? It's just not possible."

The husband said in a low tone, as though Sophie couldn't hear him, "I told you."

In unison, the two got up.

"But you haven't finished your wine yet." Sophie felt her cheeks flush.

"Never mind that," said the woman. She took her husband's arm and hustled him off.

Sophie watched them cross the piazza, avoiding the pigeons without unlinking their hands or even breaking stride. She drank another glass of the red wine straight down and suddenly it was warm enough to throw off her shawl, though the palm leaves above her head swayed in an evening breeze. It was quite dark now. It must be very late. But the café was a bright oasis, cheerful with its yellow umbrellas and red chairs and gleaming café lights strung like swaying stars.

Her phone glinted on the table. If she turned it on, and he had answered, her life could simply flow back into its predictable and pleasing path. She'd finish her troublesome article, send it off by the deadline, and fly home to Boston in under a week. Resume her job and her marriage, her life. Surely that would be best.

But if he hadn't answered, or if she just didn't turn her phone back on to find out, she might stay here, in Milan, or maybe she'd go on to Rome and see those miraculous walls, or maybe travel on to Athens or Istanbul instead.

She took a final swig of the wine, finishing it off, and spun the empty glass between her fingers. She'd have to find new work of course. She'd miss her maple desk at the travel agency, its neat piles of paper and slanting sunlight from the tall window pouring over her in the mornings as she drank her coffee. But she'd freelance, she'd wear green heels and drink red wine instead, alone or with others, in cafes like this one each night. She would not be disturbed about being tall. She would forget about being lonely and just be alone. She would be a different woman living an entirely different life.

It was all possible, if she wanted it. She touched the phone with her index finger, gently, smelling the night nicotiana drifting over the piazza in the warm breeze.

It was past eleven on Friday morning and Sophie had missed her nine am deadline. But she could still turn the design show article in late, if she hurried. She'd made a start on it; it was nearly done. She looked out the window, pressing her fingers against the sheet glass, warm already from the sun. Dust motes floating in a column from the window over to the bed.

Instead of hurrying, she dressed slowly. Nothing looked right in the multiple hotel mirrors and she piled rejected outfits on the bed. At the bottom of her suitcase she found a pale silk shirt with cap sleeves, something her sister had given her years ago. She'd stuck it in at the last moment, thinking it might be hot. She put it on and smoothed the pale pink silk over her waist. She thought about calling her sister. They hadn't talked for a long time. Months, or maybe a year. Her phone was in her bag on the night table. She pushed a discarded scarf aside and dug out the phone.

But talking with Lucia was always stressful. Sophie sat on the edge of the bed, the phone in her lap. Lucia was so energetic and enterprising and yet easy-going at the same time. Everyone loved Lucia, even her father, who certainly should have loved his real child the best. Lucia was only a half-sister, after all, and Sophie his true daughter. She fiddled with her contact list, scrolling up and down. Lucia was listed under Lucy, her real name, but she hated it and refused to talk if you used it.

Sophie felt her stomach clench up, though she hadn't even had breakfast yet. She dropped the phone back into her purse. Lucia's name was just too close to the space once occupied by Martin on her contact list, she told herself. But she knew it was way more than that.

Grabbing the last clothes from her open suitcase, she tossed aside a jacket and pulled on a linen pencil skirt, celery green, and stared at herself in the full-length mirror. She was tall, and pleasingly pastel, and she pulled her hair up into a messy knot on the very top of her head, making herself taller still, like the women in Stockholm did. She put on the green high heels.

Downstairs and outside, the switch from air conditioning to June noonday heat was startling. She wandered until she found an air-conditioned and dark café, and sat for an hour, drinking espresso and pretending to read her book. When the noisy lunch crowd barged in, she paid and walked on. Without reaching any conclusions, she had reached the train station. And why not? It would be much cooler this afternoon at one of the islands on the lake. She bought a ticket to Stresa and got on the train. She pulled out her novel and sat with it on her lap, but she didn't open it; she dozed, half listening to the young American couple across from her bicker about whose parents they would visit first at the August holidays.

After reaching Stresa, and passing through the town, the streets almost familiar to her now, but silenced by the afternoon break, she got on the ferry and when she got off, on Isola Madre again, she felt strangely happy. Energized by the cool breeze, she decided to take the grassy path into the center of the island, to the clearing sprinkled with feverfew and flanked by tall palms. The path wandered, half in sunlight and half in shade, and so green in its many incarnations, emerald and cedar and viridian. Every so often her way was interrupted with a marble statue, encrusted with lichen. She examined each one. After a time, she took off the shoes, which were certainly impractical for this sort of path, and strolled barefoot, her feet enjoying the cool tickle of damp grass and crushed flowers. Through the trees, beyond, she could hear others walking and talking as they strolled on other paths, but no one came along her way and this made her happier still.

When she grew tired, Sophie sat on a granite bench in the dappled light and smelled the pale roses, overblown and spicy. The ruffled petals slid through her fingers, and she imagined a pink velvet sofa under a tall window, warm with billowy cushions. She yawned, and closed her eyes for just a moment.

When she opened her eyes, a wind had come up and as she noticed this, the sun was blotted out by a dark cloud and goose bumps sprang up on her bare arms. She must have slept, though she never did that in a public place. She looked around quickly, startled at herself, but there was no one to see her. She got up and walked on.

The wind grew stronger; the trees made alarming cracking sounds. Needles swirled down from the pines. Palm leaves rattled, blown inside out by the wind, which plastered her skirt to her legs. She walked faster, toward where she'd heard voices last and came out into a clearing, in which a house or really a palace rose, like some building out of a fairy tale. The wind whipped her hair over her mouth and the sky was a violent purple and the trees were raining pinecones with sharp barbed edges. She ran up the granite stairs and onto the portico and turned at the sound of hail pounding down, tiny round stones of ice crashing onto the pavers and bending down the marguerites and blowing petunias into shredded streamers.

She was not alone on the porch. Two men, younger men, Italian, cigarettes in their fingers, paused in their conversation. They stared at her.

"Hello," she said. "Buon giorno, I mean."

For a moment no one answered. Then one of the men nodded to her and said in English, "Hello. You're escaping the rain, as are we. Can I offer you my jacket?"

She was shivering, the skin on her bare arms puckered and red with cold. Her silk blouse, she thought, must be transparent.

"Oh no. Thank you. You are too kind." Flustered, she backed away to the far side of the porch and stared out over the lawn and into the trees, so the men could return to their conversation.

The storm roiled overhead, blowing clouds and tossing branches. Rain slanted down, sharp and cold. She saw him then, for the first time, a flash running from tree to tree, a child, out there in the storm. She turned to the men but they were absorbed, speaking in low tones so she couldn't pick up their words. When she looked back into the darkness of the trees, the child was gone.

She went inside, though even there the wide open windows with no glass meant the wind streamed in with a wailing noise, flinging her wet hair about, and causing the glass chandelier high above to tinkle and chime. She went from dark room to dark room, each with huge wide windows letting the storm come in and inhabit the house, so there was no difference really between indoors and out. This is what it must have been like, she thought, centuries ago, homes subject to the elements, with no electric or heat or even window glass.

Standing in the center of a huge room, under a huge chandelier with colored crystals clinking, she remembered a time, shortly after her father remarried, when they all went on a family vacation to a cabin in the mountains above Santa Cruz. The cabin, built of logs, was hidden deep in the shadowy redwoods and damp inside, dripping indoors as the rain poured outside each afternoon. She was supposed to play with Lucy/Lucia, keep her amused. "You're the older sister now Sophie, I expect you to be responsible." She hadn't though. She'd ignored Lucia, and buried her face in a book, which wasn't even engrossing. She'd felt like the forgotten elder sister in some fairy story, left to die of loneliness on her own while everyone made a fuss about the new and beautiful daughter, the entertaining and amiable Lucia.

Lightning was cracking now, lighting up the rooms and shaking the floor, and there seemed to be no one else in the house at all, as though they'd all taken the last ferry and she was truly alone in the palace, alone perhaps on the whole island. Uneasy despite herself, Sophie ran down the stairs and found even the porch empty, the men gone, and only rain and silence in the courtyard. The granite statues were darkened and the ivy dripped, flattened over the black stones.

Then she saw him again, a flash of silver as he ran from tree to tree, the child. She stared into the silent, wet trees and saw him peek out. She beckoned but he shook his head and so she stepped out, into the fierce rain. It poured onto her head and shoulders, drenching her instantly. The rain was cold but the winds skimmed oddly warm over her bare arms. She shoved her bangs out of her eyes and entered the trees, threading through the dark trunks. She ducked, avoiding the branches bending with the forceful winds. The air was thick and smelled of water, wood smoke, pine needles, and decay.

She felt a tug at her skirt and there was the boy, his dark hair plastered to his neck. He tugged again and laughed and ran ahead.

The boy kept darting along, then turning back to meet her eyes. He definitely wanted her to follow. Perhaps someone was hurt; perhaps the child needed help. Why was he here alone? He was young, only six or seven she thought. He was leading her away from the empty palace and deep into the stylized wilderness, the romantic wild garden of tangled vines and swaying palms and oaks all mixed together. A garden built in the English style, or what passed for it in 19th century Italy. There were sharp acorns on the path, stabbing into her bare feet. She clutched her soaked green heels in one hand and hoped they wouldn't be ruined.

The storm should have passed over, as the winds were strong, but instead it seemed to be sitting right over the center of the island. Sophie pushed aside some drenched branches and realized she stood on a cliff, overlooking the lake, which flowed vast and green and ended in the Alps, crowned with snow and roiling clouds. Where was the child? What if he fell? What if she fell? She took a step back. The earth was mossy here and crumbly and smelled of wet lichen. She wondered if the boy was teasing her, luring her away from the house and safety. But that was a strange thought; the child was in danger surely, not she.

She could not see the boy anywhere, so she retraced her steps, the only sound the pattering of the slowing rain on soaked leaves. Her skirt was so wet it clung to her thighs and her arms were white and chilled. The boy was gone, as though he'd never been, and she was alone again.

Down at the pier, she told the uninterested woman in the ticket booth about the lost child and got on the next ferry. When she turned for a last look at the island, she thought she would see him once more, peering out, perhaps, from one of the giant festooned pots. But she did not. Maybe, she thought, she hadn't seen him at all. That seemed more and more likely as the ferry, and then the train, carried her along. Back in Milan, she took a long hot shower in the hotel's marble bath until she finally stopped shivering, scrubbing herself with rosemary soap, water pouring over her cheeks like tears.

The weekend over, her deadline met with an adequate article emailed in late, Sophie got into a cab and headed to the airport, staring aimlessly at the dun apartment buildings as they passed through Milan's suburbs. She hadn't turned her phone on until this morning. It sat on her lap now, glowing messages piled up, filling her box. Scrolling down she saw seventeen were from Martin.

The cab pulled into the airport and the driver got out and opened the trunk to pull out her bag. She continued to sit in the back seat, with its grimy black leather and smell of cigarette smoke. She wondered if travel opened the mind or just made one even more of a stranger to oneself. She thought about all the people she'd helped to travel in her job. Most of them repeat customers at her firm, year after year. Some returning to the same island resort or European city, over and over. Others going always somewhere new. As though a trip were an acquisition. I've been here and here and there. Peru one year, China the next. Machu Picchu. The Great Wall.

She rolled down the window and called to the cab driver. "Take me back to the train station."

He shrugged and tossed his cigarette butt on the tar. As he started to drive, he turned up the radio and the sound of urgent voices filled the cab, speaking insistently in fast Italian of something she couldn't quite catch or understand.

An hour later, she paid the driver and entered the train station and boarded the next train headed north. She didn't read, just gazed out the window, watching the blur of colors as apartment buildings gave way to fields and orchards with pink blossoms whirred into deep rose as they whipped by. On the ferry back to the island, she began to think about him, the boy, more urgently.

Real or imagined, there had certainly been a storm, violent rain, warm winds. The palace open to the weather. Strange almost menacing men. Were these things all connected in some story she had yet to comprehend? She felt she'd glimpsed something outside her sphere, something to take back with her if she could just put it together and understand. Not an acquisition to be placed in front of others on her living room table--yes, that's the paperweight I got in Venice--more like a fierce glowing coal to hoard inside, something to embody the yearning.

On the island, she passed up the stairs in the hot sun, then she walked the cool shady paths until she'd circled the island twice. She walked the interior paths, deep in shade, damp seeping through her sandals. She walked the whole afternoon until the sun sank and the shadows turned violet and a wind kicked up over the lake, snapping the flag high on the ferry landing pole. She saw only tourists strolling, and a couple whispering and kissing on a bench together, and no children at all.

She returned to Stresa on the nearly empty ferry, but not to Milan. She booked herself into a pension in the old town and sat by the tall window, watching the sunset spread its glow over the lake and eating dry cookies dipped in lukewarm tea. She thought about Lucia and what she might say to her, if they could actually put aside their competition and simply talk.

In the morning, she returned to the island. On the second day, she never found the boy, but instead she found, at the end of one of the longest paths, just by the lake where the water rushed up in soft waves onto the sand, a stone ship only one foot long, a viking ship with its dragon front and intricate scrolled sides. Variegated ivy curled down its sides and nameless white flowers with a powerful scent spiraled up into the air. A tiny ship for explorers, hidden here in the moss, nearly lost but not quite.

The third morning, she felt anticipation. And she was rewarded, as soon as she'd landed, the ferry bumping and squealing against the pier. She saw the boy, just where she'd hoped to glimpse him before, behind the huge terra cotta pots.

She followed him into the woods, stepping on soft thick moss, warm in the heat of the day. The boy began to run and she ran too, pulling off her shoes and sweater and laughing at the feel of wind hitting her cheeks. They reached the center of the island, a place with no other tourists, where the humid air smelled of earth and water. The boy pointed, and she stopped, breathing hard, and then she saw it too, a bird, a strange and wonderful bird, with a red patch on the back of its head, deep green feathers down its back, and a speckled breast. It ran before them, singing a wonderful song and though it never flew, still they couldn't seem to catch it. They tracked it all day, she and the boy laughing, the bird cocking its head and seeming to wait for them, running ahead and hiding under branches, then reappearing, its beak golden in the afternoon sun. They chased the bird until the sun sank and the song ceased and then Sophie looked around and the bird and the boy and the light were gone.

Three days later, Sophie got out of the cab at the Milan airport and paid the driver. She dragged her suitcase with its one broken wheel along behind her. Inside were three new pairs of heels, lavender and silver and one spangled with glittering sequins. In her hand, she had her phone. She wondered if she would call Martin first, or Lucia. She wondered what they would understand when she told them about the boy and the bird. She walked toward her plane, waiting on the hot pavement of the runway, and a flock of small finches rose into the air chattering and chirping, their green and gold feathers glinting. They were too far away in an instant, settling onto a magnolia tree at the far end of the runway. She watched them for a long moment, despite the hot wind ruffling her hair, wishing she could hold out her hand and one might land on her outstretched finger.

THE FORGOTTEN GARDEN

Italy, 1933

The garden had been forgotten for so long that no one remembered its name, and Isabelle was the first person to disturb it for many years. She had arrived at the big house in a flurry of luggage, leather bags strapped with bright fasteners, and she entered the double front doors still wearing her airy wide-brimmed hat, trimmed with fluttering silk. Jane and Evan, the only two servants left at the house, exchanged glances, and then stared at the floor with its wide oak planks, polished with beeswax by Jane, monthly, on her hands and knees. Isabelle hadn't glanced at the floor; she'd just pushed open the French doors and exclaimed and rushed out onto the terrace, disappearing down the path on the farthest side, where the hedges, still clipped by Evan once a summer, grew lush and so thick she just vanished from their view. It was only later, much later, that they learned she'd found the garden on that very first afternoon.

But many other events intervened before that discovery. That first evening, Isabelle had come down to dinner properly, wearing a satin gown with cap sleeves and a glittering brooch shaped like a spray of tulips above her left breast. David, the owner of this house, was there with her, of course, properly suited in grey and black with a crisp white shirt Jane had laundered and folded and stroked with her red fingers before placing it carefully in his armoire. She'd raised him, more or less, as his father was always in London and his mother preferred riding horses to tending a child and neither of them needed to bother and so they had not. That was the strange way of it, but she didn't mind filling in as Davy had always been a sweet child and her one daughter had, by then, married and moved south. She'd always known she should keep a tighter rein on her feelings, but he'd nestled into her heart and so here she still was, though Davy hardly needed her anymore and didn't seem to remember those long afternoons when she watched him roll about in the tall grass or squelch in the mud by the pond. Off to school he'd gone and returned quiet, near a stranger, if such a thing were possible. She tried to explain her hurt feelings to Evan in the evenings when they shared a glass of sherry together before bed, but he just advised her to be practical and guard her emotions and what use was that as they were already spilled or spent or out of the stable or any other old saying one wanted to invoke.

That first dinner with Isabelle made Jane anxious. It didn't go as it ought. The food had been fine, beef roast following a soufflé in the French style made of good cheddar and green onions. And a dessert of berries topped with fresh whipped cream. The new wife had eaten it all and seemed pleased. But when dinner was done, she'd said in a clear voice, so loud that Jane couldn't help but think she was meant to hear, that this solid English food was lovely but so old fashioned and of course they'd have to engage a new cook if they meant to entertain. They might be marooned here in Italy, but they had to keep up with the trends at home or people would certainly laugh. Davy had simply nodded and picked up one of his new wife's slender hands and Jane had to stand there shocked and stiff-faced and contemplate a new person taking over in her clean kitchen. Which had occurred only a few short weeks later. And the changes hadn't stopped there. Within a month there were six new servants roaming the stairs, two from Paris, three from Rome, and only one from back home in Shropshire. Even the furniture in the dining room and master bedroom had been hauled out to the stucco barns, new tables and chairs and sideboards imported and installed, and the carpets had been rolled up and taken away entirely. The house was different, lighter and livelier, so that Evan complained he had headache nearly every evening.

Davy was happy, that much Jane could see and so she held her tongue, even though Isabelle disappeared every afternoon right after lunch and didn't come home again until tea. Often she returned somewhat disheveled, her hat hanging down her back by its silk ties and her cheeks pink from the sun. Davy didn't seem to notice, he was working so hard those days, and his accountant kept him locked in the study for all the long hot afternoon hours.

"Where does she go?" asked Evan one evening, staring into his sherry glass as though the prism of light, examined so many evenings, had acquired new interest.

Jane shook her head and the sherry in her glass trembled. But after that, she wondered more, because if even Evan had noticed, it was surely odd and she wasn't wrong to wonder if something were out of place. She was so used to everything being the same, everything being orderly. She was so used to following orders. As a child, her father had her knitting stockings to sell at the Monday market, and then he'd apprenticed her out as a kitchen maid, and after he'd died she'd just stayed on and risen to nursemaid and then housekeeper, but always someone else telling her what to do. It was unsettling to consider going outside the normal way of things and doing something new at this point in her days. But she made herself do it, one Tuesday afternoon, the sun gleaming hot but storm clouds piling over the terraced hills. It would rain by evening.

She followed Isabelle, who was flying along the path beyond the terrace. She had to walk fast as she tried to keep up and yet not be seen coming on behind.

It was actually lovely to be out of doors in the middle of a summer afternoon, just walking in the back gardens. She hadn't been out here in years, not since the gardeners had been let go. She was always busy in the kitchen or dusting at this hour. She found herself touching a spiky leaf or a silky petal, and lifted a heavy full-blown rose to smell. But then she had to hurry because Isabelle was not viewing the lilies, but sweeping past them, her long scarves gathering grass stains and damp spots as she went.

Jane was getting tired, her legs ached and her ankle cracked at each step. Isabelle had disappeared far ahead. She wondered if she should keep going. Isabelle might have gone anywhere; how would she ever find her? The gardens were extensive and where they ended, the wilderness began. Though Jane had lived right here for many years, she still thought of Italy, outside the estate grounds, as wild, outside the regular realm of things.

But she kept going and then she heard a sound, a child laughing. When she peered through the wide-open gate of the farthest garden on the very edge of the estate, there was Isabelle lying flat on the grass and beside her a small boy, barely five years surely, chased butterflies as Isabelle laughed.

Jane sat down on a bench just outside the garden, hidden by the overgrown vines and cedar hedge and thought. Who could this boy be? Why didn't Isabelle bring him into the house? How like Davy the boy seemed, so carefree and demanding.

In the end, Jane returned to the house before Isabelle and said nothing, even to Evan. This seemed somehow a weighty matter, a secret not to be penetrated by simply asking. She would have to puzzle it out, and she felt that the ultimate answer would be worth the effort and the waiting.

Six years passed in this odd way. Jane would follow Isabelle on the first day of each month and the pattern was unchanging. Twelve times a year, Jane watched as Davy's wife and this boy played and lounged in the farthest forgotten garden. A garden that no longer had a name anyone could recall. Isabelle never ordered the new gardeners to open the gates and weed or prune those roses, but kept them working trimming the lawns at the front of the house and shearing the box into spiral topiaries to line the gravel drive. And Jane never spoke to Isabelle nor to anyone about what she watched.

Only the child changed, growing taller, his games growing ever quieter. Davy was away more and more. A child of his own had never come and never would, for Jane knew that now they kept separate bedrooms. Isabelle was always silent and secretive about all parts of her life. Against the custom she had no personal maid, and even bathed herself and dressed her own hair. But Jane had heard her once, weeping in her room behind the closed door.

So when the next war came, it wasn't surprising really that Davy was always in London and never came over, even in the spring when he had always escaped the cold fogs and enjoyed the blooming of the blue and white iris under the olive trees. After two years of the war, the French cook was sent away and Jane had her kitchen back again. All the young men from the village went to fight. Evan was too old and lame to go, but so many didn't come back and then some did, and hobbled around on their wooden legs or sat alone in the mothers' dark kitchens and cried for days and days. The world had gone all topsy-turvy and Jane couldn't understand. For some reason she went more and more to the garden, following Isabelle, breaking her rule of once a month, and so she saw them the afternoon they argued.

She couldn't hear the words, but the boy was fourteen now and old enough to want to follow the rest to the wars, but too young for his mother to be forced to let him go. If he had a mother. Jane had wondered so many times if Isabelle were his mother; it seemed she must be, yet why did they only meet in this way?

The boy didn't play with his bat or arrows or net, just sulked, and Isabelle, for the first time, returned from the garden early, her hat jammed on her head, tears gathering in her blue eyes.

The next month the boy was not there. Jane watched as Isabelle sat alone in the empty garden, on the damp grass by the late roses. After a time, she walked in a wavering circle and seemed to listen for the boy, or perhaps she listened to the rustle of early fallen leaves as they grazed her boots. She walked round and round the dry fountain with its cherub gazing skyward and Isabelle gazed skyward too, to where a pair of sparrows winged back and forth in their acrobatics, and beyond, it seemed, to the fringe of clouds at the edge of the sky.

The boy never returned. Jane knew this, because like Isabelle, she went many times to the garden and walked and waited. After twelve months passed, Isabelle went to the garden no more. The gate rusted shut in the winter rains. Only Jane went to the garden, squeezing past the frozen gate through the scratchy cedar branches. Perhaps she went because the boy might come back and what if there was no one there to meet him? Isabelle just stayed in the house and read a book in the study or sketched by the fire or sometimes just gazed out her bedroom window for many hours at the rain.

Then one spring morning nearing noon, Isabelle came downstairs in traveling skirts and a blue velvet hat with a chiffon bow under her chin. "Tell the master," she said to Jane, "I have gone."

"Gone where?" said Jane, "what shall I tell him?"

Isabelle shook her head and the fragile bow trembled like a butterfly might. "I know you have followed me, so I know you already know why." She examined the drafty hall once more, then went out the door.

But Jane didn't know why, not really, and she wondered on the mystery for many months and then for many years. Davy stayed on in London, the war went on and then ended, but Isabelle and the boy never returned. The garden stayed forgotten and the neglected pale roses bloomed, it seemed, only for Jane's own pleasure and for no one else at all.

THE INTERVIEW

The abandoned villa had blank windows and broken shutters and glorious gilt scrolls above its double doors. Cassandra could see all this by pushing aside the tangle of overgrown vines climbing up and over the wrought iron fence. The ivy leaves were wet with morning dew and spattered dark ovals across her silk blouse. As she was on her way to a job interview, this was inconvenient.

She brushed at the water drops and smeared them. She'd just have to let them dry and hope they didn't leave spots. She didn't exactly wear silk often, so how should she know if it would spot or not? She wished she could forget about the interview entirely. Wouldn't it be lovely to just walk in through the villa's slightly ajar iron gate, step through the tall grasses, even though they'd soak her skirt, and sit in the morning sun on the terrace with its brick floor, cracked terra cotta pots, and that grey cat peering around the edge of the building. For a moment she wanted to sit on that terrace so badly her eyes burned and watered. She turned abruptly and went on down the sidewalk, unsteady with her leather-soled flats on the slick cobbles.

On her left, the lake stretched out, calm in the morning sun and a lovely silvery blue streaked with pink. So welcoming in the summer sun. She wondered what it would be like in winter, whether it froze over and one could skate. A few early tourists strolled toward the boat landing, waiting every few steps for one woman who used a cane. Three policemen or possibly parking attendants lounged against the vans in the parking lot, laughing loudly. It was a good morning apparently, for everyone else.

Cass glanced at her watch. She had a half hour to kill. She'd caught the earliest train from Milan because she had no idea if the trains ran on time here in Italy, though she suspected they did not. But in fact she'd arrived in Stresa four minutes early. It was a city, but a small and compact one, with two central squares and one main street, and some winding roads that were narrow as paths and lined with extremely bright flowers in pots.

She noticed a café across the street and the waitress, standing at the door, sun on her face, smiled at her. So she went in and ordered a coffee and two cookies and asked to have them at the table on the sidewalk, though she knew it would cost her four times as much. The waitress looked surprised, but she smiled again as she set the hot espresso on the table and went back to standing in the doorway, a pleased look on her face. She must have had a good evening, maybe a successful date with one of those policemen across the square by the ticket counter. She was covertly watching them. Cass watched too and drank her coffee and ate her cookies and wished she had two more but she was embarrassed to ask for them. She gathered up her bag and left the café, heading toward the hospital.

At the gate, she almost turned around. But she'd come all this way. She should go inside. She should try. She straightened her skirt, which had slid around her waist so the zipper was at her right hip, and tucked in her slippery blouse. She didn't have a mirror to check her teeth, but she hoped they were okay. She walked up to the large double doors, painted a brilliant glossy white, and paused, staring at a pot of unnaturally pink geraniums. A large pot, one that came up to her waist and the geraniums cascaded in full health upwards and also down the sides. It was meant to cheer up the families, she guessed, when they came to visit.

She took a deep breath and pulled open the heavy door and stepped into a foyer, cool and dim and decorated with paintings of Greek and Roman ruins, which seemed a strange choice.

"What are you doing here?" said a female voice. "It's not the hour for visits." She spoke in English, having judged correctly that Cass did not belong here in this lakeside town.

A second person, an efficient looking woman with charcoal hair slicked down to her head clicked up on very high heels.

Cass wanted to step back out the door, but she didn't. "I'm here for the job," she said too loudly. "I have an appointment for an interview."

"Oh that," said the woman with the heels. She tapped a foot, seeming to admire her own slim ankle above the slick patent leather. "Come this way then."

Cass clumped along behind, feeling thirty pounds overweight and wishing she'd thought to get her hair cut or at least tied it back.

You couldn't have hair falling on the patients. Not that she'd have anything to do with patients. That wasn't in the job description.

They entered a long hallway and the woman pointed to a very modern black leather chair and her stern look indicated sit, so Cass lowered herself onto the strange chair and put her tapestry bag down onto the floor beside her. The woman disappeared through a set of swinging double doors. It was very quiet in this hospital, no beepers or buzzers or disgruntled children or tired mothers, no one at all actually. She wondered why she had thought a job like this would be good for her, at this point in her life. Back in London, she'd read the newspaper ad with such excitement. A job in the Italian Lakes; she could live in an apartment and she could have a tiny garden of her own or at least some potted plants on a balcony. It would be quiet, that would be the thing, and it would be not London. Because whatever she did, not London was what she needed right now.

She'd packed her bag before she'd even emailed and she'd flown to Paris before she'd even heard back. Then she'd caught the night train to Milan, sure that this interview was a sign that her life would now take a positive turn. What had she been thinking?

A man dressed in a black tuxedo-like suit came to the door. "Miss Cassandra O'Leary?"

Cass got to her feet. Should she have worn a long dress? What kind of hospital was this? "Pleased to meet you," she said and held out a hand but he had already turned away and probably didn't see it. She followed him down a corridor, feeling like a scolded child, and he gestured to a waiting room, lined with green chairs. There was also a sofa of the sinking sort on the far end, but she ignored that. She sat on one of the stiff chairs and wondered where the other job candidates were and how long she'd have to wait. After ten minutes, in which she imagined the coffee and cookies again, and promised herself more after this ordeal, a woman came through, her face flushed. She looked around at the empty room, as though confused and went out.

The tuxedo fellow reappeared. "You may come in now," he said.

Cass trailed him into an office, very small and completely white. Even the file folders piled on the shelves were white, with dove grey writing in block print. There was a small window, looking out on the car park. The room was hot, sun shining in, and Cass sat on the plastic chair he offered her. He went out and she waited. It was really quite hot and she felt a drop of sweat trickle down her neck.

The woman with the heels she'd already seen entered and sat on the other plastic chair behind the desk. She looked cool, even cold, and her hair looked wet, though it was probably styling gel. Cass wondered why she didn't say she was the potential new boss when they'd met before.

"I always do that," said the woman, reading her face correctly. "I can learn more about you from that quick meeting than a half day interview."

"I see," said Cass. What she thought was, what have you learned?

"I've decided you'll suit," said the woman, pulling a white folder down and opening it in front of her on the desk. "Will starting a week from Thursday be appropriate for you? With the festival this week, there's no point in starting earlier."

"I suppose, I mean, yes, of course," said Cass. "Yes."

"Perfect," said the woman, snapping the file shut.

"But I'll need to find somewhere to live."

"Ahh," said the woman, a slight crease forming between her penciled brows. "There's an HR department to deal with all that. Here's their card." She stood up.

Cass stood too and picked up her bag. "Can I ask a question though? What will my duties be exactly, what will my day be like?"

The woman looked pained and put a hand on the door. "You'll take care of the files for the patients' records. It's all organized; we have a wonderful system. There will be no problems or difficulties. Maureen, who had the position before you, left everything in perfect order."

"Why did she leave?" said Cass.

"You'll understand that's not something I'm permitted to reveal," said the woman. She left and Cass felt like she had clicked her high heels together, though of course she hadn't.

For a time, two months actually, the job was perfect. Cass drank espresso every morning, walked the six blocks to the hospital from the flat she'd rented, filed and typed in a quiet room with a large window and three white desks, though she was the only one working there. Through the open door, she'd glimpse nurses trudging by in their sturdy white shoes, and once in a while, through the window, she'd see the actual patients as they wandered the grounds, usually arm in arm on a day of sun and warm breezes.

The filing and the quiet were boring, but in a wonderful way, after London. She'd had a job in a hectic advertising agency, assistant to the head of PR putting together ad campaigns for airline companies. She'd been a good assistant, clever and bright, at least that's what her boss had said when she had one of their annual evaluations. And he took plenty of her ideas and wove them into ads, so she'd thought that meant a promotion would be hers soon. She had a graphic arts degree, after all. But the promotion was slow in coming and one evening after work, when they'd had a couple of beers together, she'd told him what she thought, that he was using her. And just like that, he'd fired her. And blacklisted her, so that months of no work had followed, until she'd been forced to realize she had no future at any of the London firms and there was really nothing she could do about it.

But the worst part, the part she couldn't stand to remember, was what she'd done to him. She'd called his wife, one night she knew he was out with a client, and told her he was having an affair, though she had no idea if that were the case and no evidence for it at all. She'd made her voice sound sincere and helpful. Later, she'd heard from a gossiping mutual friend that the wife left him and took the twins and even the family cat, a striped tiger with a shortened tail. For a moment, after hanging up the phone, she'd felt thrilled, but since then she'd only felt sick, somewhere deep beneath her breastbone, in a way which seemed it wouldn't disappear. So when she'd seen the ad for this job, she'd answered immediately.

But now, when Cass stared at the file in her hand, she realized there was no longer any question. She'd been an accountant for a period of three years just after art school, before she'd gotten her job in the agency; she knew how to read a spreadsheet and how to add. The hospital, or someone in the hospital, was routinely stealing the patients' money. Right out of their private bank accounts. Small amounts, month by month, but adding up to quite a lot over time. The question was, what was she to do about it? Was this why Maureen had left?

She put the file back into the drawer, shut the drawer, locked it, and put on her raincoat. It was just past dusk on an early fall evening and she walked the few blocks to her flat slowly as people hurried past her, on their way home to families and dinners and tumblers of red wine.

She climbed the three flights of stairs, reaching the top in the dark as the timed light switched off. Inside her flat, the air felt still and blank and the sofa loomed grey in the dim light. Cass shoved open the sliding door and went out onto the balcony, where she'd planted four pots--marigolds, cosmos, bougainvillea and fuchsia. The bright flowers clashed wildly, and she would sit out here on the long evenings and drink exactly half a bottle of wine, glass after glass, using the tiny crystal aperitif glass she'd purchased from the second hand shop by the train station. This was her home now; she went walking on the lake path each morning before work. She bought her groceries every other day from the shop at the corner. On weekends, she attended the local fairs and farm markets or took small sightseeing excursions to gardens around the lake. She was planning a visit to Milan even, before the Christmas holidays, to go to the art museum and see the cathedral and the castle. She was living here, in Italy, but really it was more like being a permanent tourist, if she were honest, knowing no one, responsible to no one. It suited her and now this horrible knowledge was ruining it all.

If she let it. She dropped into the chair and stared into the dusk. What difference did it really make, after all? All the patients came from extremely rich families. They were the castaways, the irredeemable ones who would never go back to a normal life.

The families knew it and rarely visited. The patients knew it and slumped on the garden benches or in the hallways or TV room watching the same film over and over with a vacant look. On their best days they wandered in the garden until the nurse rounded them up and sat them down to dinner. Their families opened accounts for them, encouraged by the hospital, but the patients had no need for money and nothing to spend it on.

Cass plucked a dead marigold head off the plant and thought that it was getting cold on the balcony. Her plants would have to retreat inside soon. Seeing the patients, their strange half lives so repetitious and surely monotonous, and so lonely, of course at first she'd been horrified, then compassionate, then just tired, but she'd grown accustomed to it and after all, what else could be done? They'd released one patient in his brother's care and he'd returned in two weeks so panicked and glad to be back that it had turned her whole vision upside down. These were people who wanted to be inside, who couldn't be out. What use did they have for money? And their rich families who had abandoned them, they'd never even notice, they never did notice the small drip of extra charges which added up, over time.

How silent the woman had been, the wife, only the sound of her breathing coming over the phone. Surely, Cass had thought many times, she wouldn't have believed her if it hadn't been true, if she hadn't already had suspicions. She'd thought about it, of course, on so many nights drinking her tiny glasses of wine in this very chair. Had it been wrong or right, had she been vindicated or vindictive?

And now this. Why couldn't life just leave her alone? One couldn't escape the usual questions of whether you pass by the homeless person or drop a dollar in the jar, but this? She didn't want to be responsible, she didn't want to choose. Didn't want moral dilemmas or philosophic decisions or this awfulness in her chest and stomach. What a pitiful excuse of a person she was, really. She poured more wine into her glass, though she'd already passed her quota.

If she told someone, who would she choose to tell? Who was stealing the money or was it all of them in it together? She'd likely lose her job, she'd lose her whole new life here, and it wasn't so easy for a failed graphic artist with "difficult" stamped on her resume to find a job. It could even be dangerous. And her life here, it might not be too much, but she loved sitting by the friendly waitress in the morning and drinking her coffee, and sipping her wine as she fondled her plants in the evening, and if she told, it would all be upended. Where would she go then? The world was so huge, but each place was so wrong. Nowhere else was home anymore.

She got up and went back inside and switched on a light, then switched it off again. She didn't want to be in this position, but what if she stayed silent? What would happen to her if she colluded? What sort of person would she turn out to be? One bad decision seemed like cause for regret, but two in one life seemed like a slide into something. She imagined herself an old woman, walking down a long empty street, the smell of talcum powder and dank water and her own old skin when she lifted a hand to brush her hair from her face.

And what if they realized already that she knew? Were they testing her? Who were they anyway? What had really happened to Maureen? How her head ached and ached. She would be forty-five in just two months; she was in her prime, and yet somehow she hadn't learned how to be herself yet, in her own skin, certain.

Two nights later, Cass decided she needed to talk things over with someone. From her seat on the balcony, she watched a swallow flit among the leaves at the top of the olive tree opposite her building. The sky was twilight blue and the air still warm from the day and caressing. The wine in her glass soothing. But who? She knew no one in this town. Up until now, that had seemed a wonderful freedom. It hadn't bothered her at all to be alone. She didn't want to confide in anyone at the hospital, so who?

She did know one person, she realized, sort of. The woman at the coffee shop, who made her double espresso and placed three cookies on her saucer each morning, without asking. That was a kind of familiarity. Sufficient, she thought.

The next morning, Cass walked faster than usual, and entered the cafe so quickly she nearly ran into an older woman exiting, her bag of cookies clutched in thin fingers.

"Angelica," Cass said, glad that she knew the woman's name, glad she'd learned enough Italian. "Can I ask you something? Something important?"

Angelica looked surprised and frowned, but nodded. "Let me get your coffee going," she said. Just then two policemen came through the door, their burly shoulders filling the tiny room. Angelica handed her the espresso and turned to the men.

"But," said Cass. Angelica was smiling and talking to the men with a burst of Italian that Cass couldn't possibly follow. She backed out the door and sat down at her regular table, though it was getting chilly in the mornings now. She hadn't seen the police come inside before. They generally stayed in the parking lot, talking. What had brought them out now, so inconveniently? She gulped the hot coffee. Angelica had even forgotten her cookies. Her coffee emptied, Cass lingered but the policemen didn't seem to be leaving, so finally she felt conspicuous and she left. At the corner she turned to look back. One of the policemen was standing at the door, sipping his coffee, and watching her, wasn't he?

A week passed and another, and Cass thought about the files and avoided thinking about the files and at night she wasn't sleeping well at all. In front of her mirror, that morning, she'd been startled to see the face of a much older woman looking back at her. She'd known then that whatever she decided, or refused to decide, would be written there in tiny creases of amazement and concern on her face and there was no escape from that.

At noon on her lunch break stroll the next day, she encountered a large poster plastered on the billboard of the town's main square. *Pattinaggio artistico esposizione.* A figure skating exhibition she deduced from the illustration. Despite the gusty November wind and the chilly drizzle, she stared at the poster for a long time, seeing her nine-year-old self lacing on blue skates with grey fur tops and flinging herself into twirls and jumps. Where had that exuberant girl gone? She hadn't thought about that child in years. The poster showed a young woman, her tiny red skirt blowing in the gale of her motion, her legs in an improbable aerial split.

Cass returned to work and filed patient records and penciled in appointments for the director and avoided the patients' grasping hands as she walked down the hall to the rest room and back. She tried to make that small journey as seldom as possible, now that the dreary weather kept the patients all inside instead of scattered across the lawns. They seemed happy, they were happy in here, all the nurses said so. Still, sometimes, in the night, she would wake and stare alone into the dark and wonder. How did it happen, that she was out here and they were in there? Would they exchange places one day?

The next evening after work, Cass passed by the poster again. Impulsively, she stopped and bought a ticket from the excited children at the card table set up on the corner. The exhibition was for that very night, at nine pm, in the rink outside the town. She hadn't even known there was a rink. She decided to walk, as it wasn't too far, just three kilometers and then she'd take a cab back after. Surely there would be one around. Having decided this, she skipped dinner but drank two small glasses of wine and then dressed with care. When she examined herself in the wavy mirror by the door of her apartment, she looked solemn and much too formal, so she mussed her dark hair so some slid out of the careful French knot at the back of her head, and she changed her earrings from plain gold studs to a dangling pair with green and lavender glass balls that she'd purchased after she got her first paycheck. She hadn't worn them yet; she hadn't actually gone out at night at all since she'd been here. She nodded at her improved reflection, setting the balls swaying.

Outside, she marched along the wide sidewalk and then onto the road. She had sneakers on, which wasn't perfect for her outfit, but necessary for walking so far. The road was light enough, in the blue light of evening, due to the moon, and empty, but for chattering grackles in the trees as she passed beneath. When she reached the rink, the parking lot was full of honking cars dropping off groups of teenage girls and two policemen guiding traffic. She slipped around them, showed her ticket, and entered the rink.

Inside, the air was frosty and dank, and smelled already of hot coffee and sweat. It was crowded and the din of voices echoing in the high metal rafters was like a roar in her ears. She walked to the far end, by the emergency exit, and found a seat high up on the bleachers, sufficiently far, she hoped, from the screaming girls chattering and checking their phones below. She drew her sweater tighter around her chest and thought she should have remembered this, how cold it could be in a rink, and worn a heavy coat.

The performance was late starting, of course, but when it came, it was fabulous. The skaters slipped one between the other, their skates making that scraping sound and sending up chips of ice, skirts flowing between their legs. They wore silver and pale blue and the sequins on their costumes sent a glitter of lights like a snowfall through the air, landing, it seemed on all the watchers. Even the teenage girls were hushed when the principal skater began her program, and the crowd clapped and sighed as she completed each flying jump.

When it was over, even the encore, Cass sat for a long time in her cold seat, until nearly everyone left the rink. When the janitor eyed her, she got up, clutching her sweater around her chest and went out the double doors into the dark parking lot. She felt as though thirty years had flown away and she'd been that skater again. Why had she ever stopped? She'd been good once, good enough that she'd been offered free lessons and later free coaching and an offer of tuition if she'd skate. But she'd gone to a local business college in the evenings, and got her graphic arts degree days. When the other art students went out to the bars, she had homework and she was always exhausted. There had been no time to skate. She'd settled for organizing numbers instead of leaping into space. When she'd finally landed her dream job at the ad agency, it had seemed like she'd finally have her chance. But it had all come to nothing.

There were no cabs and so she walked along the dark road back to town, stepping into the bushes when an occasional car rocketed past her, some teenager at the wheel. Eventually she reached the town, her legs tired and a blister starting on one heel.

Two weekends later, though it was cold and the end of the tourist season, Cass took the ferry to the far side of the lake and went walking in one of the famous gardens, Villa Taranto, built by a Scottish botanist in the 1800's. She took the long winding path upward, spiraling to the folly and tower at the top. Along the way, she passed plants, so many plants, each one carefully labeled in black ink that would not fade in the hot sun or winter rain. Latin names and variations were given. It was orderly and precise. But the overall effect of so many plants, one after the other, was of a collection, not a garden. An assemblage, not art. It had nothing in it of the leap. It was, she thought, getting more and more angry, a spreadsheet garden. She kept walking up, though she abandoned reading the signs. It was a stiff climb, and though it was almost winter, she shed her coat and then her sweater.

She had a dim idea that if she got to the top, if she could just look out over the lake and beyond the lake to the Alps, if she got perspective, it might translate, somehow, to her own life. Three months had passed since she'd found the files and the methodical sifting off of funds. She'd done her job, she'd told no one, she'd given out, she hoped, no clues. She'd thought it would come to her, what to do. But it hadn't, so far. She thought, as she trudged up, the chill wind off the lake tossing her hair, that it appeared she'd made a decision already just by not making one. And wasn't that what the philosophers said, about evil. It was hard to believe that she herself was that grand word or thing. She passed three children and a mother with a stroller, and a couple with canes, and a single old man striding along. She kept going, getting a little light headed. She'd forgotten to bring water.

At the top, she went over to the wrought iron fence and reached through and picked an out of season rose and raised it to her nose as she looked out over the lake. From up here, it stretched out, a flat silver sheet with tiny flecks of white like lint far away under the high mountains. She would stand here, she decided, looking at the lake, feeling the breeze rustle her hair, smelling the complexity of the rose; she would stand here until she made a decision.

She looked away from the town and the hospital toward the inhospitable mountains, and wondered what the cold at the top would feel like and if she would feel it soon or never. She stood there while the old man and the couple with canes and the children came up, exclaimed over the view, and left again. She waited, her legs aching, as dusk fell down over the lake. She imagined the lake below her frozen and herself skating on and on, past the inlets and famous gardens, on and on and on, all the way to the mountains, and then who knew, maybe beyond.

RIDING THE DOLPHIN

A dolphin is a strange symbol for a river, as it's well known they only live in the sea; that's what Walt thought before. Later, he learned one species of dolphins actually swims in the River Ganges. So maybe dolphins swam in the fresh water of the Italian Lakes once too. Or maybe the summer visitors of ancient times, who first made the grand terraced garden laid out before him, spent another part of the year by the sea, and felt right at home swimming with leaping dolphins. There was that myth, he half remembered, something about a god, and hapless men being turned into dolphins, blue and unpredictable as the sea.

Walt eyed the carved marble statue below him, in its own special sunken garden, water swirling around the dolphin's tail, as though the beast swam in a foaming current, and he felt like its blank eye stared straight at him and actually saw him. Ridiculous. It was a statue, part of a fountain, for Christ's sake. He was going crazy, that was all, bored to insanity following Julia around these blasted gardens on the border of Italy and Austria. It was her new thing, gardens and more gardens. But why was he here? Why did he follow her straight thin back anywhere?

Walt watched Julia peer through her camera lens, adjusting, always adjusting; he sighed and plunked himself down on an iron bench in the shade of some weird tree with giant white flowers. A crowd of Italian children rushed down the stone steps in the glaring light, screaming with excitement at being alive and out of the schoolroom and running in the sun, and he wondered, with extreme gloom, when he had lost his own zest for living.

Only twenty-four months ago, he'd been working on Wall Street. One of those energetic types in an expensive suit with Italian shoes, piling out of work at eight pm on a Friday night, laughing exuberantly in the bar, thrilled with the chill smell of his martini and the sight of limos black and sleek zipping out to the suburbs. He'd have one someday, and that day not too far off, so he didn't need to be envious. And the women, they were sleek too, dressed in low cut silk tops, the buttons undone and jackets removed now they were out of the office, suddenly desirable and the whole weekend opening up like fresh cut cantaloupe and giving off a musky scent that made his stomach tighten and excitement fizz in his chest.

No point in going over it, how all that had blown away like puffs of drifting fog shifting over a restless sea. He'd gone over it in his head, over and over again, and where did that lead? He'd tried to do the right thing, letting his boss's boss know about the inaccuracies, at least he thought he'd tried to do the right thing. He hadn't liked his boss much, that was also sure. Maybe it was revenge, or something more like petty resentment after all. Oh whatever, he'd been fired, flat out, not even let go. No package for him. Which had led to a year of him and his brand new wife Julia in his parents' spare bedroom and a solitary desk in their musty basement. Until Julia finished her degree in library science and promptly got a job. He was still unemployed. He knew he needed to get over it, switch careers, accept the inevitable pay cut, move on. But moving at all seemed impossible.

Walt got to his feet, feeling exhausted despite his age of thirty-five, as though he was his father, or his grandfather, ready to give up on it all. Julia was still snapping pictures and comparing the Latin names of the flowers on those iron markers with those in her guidebook. She could be here for hours.

He wandered down some shady steps, toward a greenhouse type affair that looked cool. He had some vague idea of finding the toilet. In the greenhouse, it was shady and damp; billows of huge leaves covering the glass ceiling so that it was like being in a green cave, a cave that was actually growing, bending and twining and twisting, living, in fact, as all things must. Walt shook his head. He was going quite wacko. He shoved a fern frond out of his face and walked on through.

On the other end was a door, so he walked through that too. And then he realized, without meaning to, he had gone out the exit and he couldn't get back in. Damn, she'd be mad. He felt in his pocket for his phone and remembered he'd given it to her and she'd put it in her backpack, so now he couldn't text her. He looked around for a guard. Maybe he could persuade someone to let him back in, but there was no one about, except a scrawny yellow and white cat and a thin teenager ostensibly selling postcards but filing her nails in the back of her shop, ignoring him completely. He passed her and the shop and wandered down the stone steps with the idea of sitting down by the lake. Julia would miss him and come out at some point and in the meantime he might as well get some lunch. He reached in his pocket and pulled out a five euro note. Hmm. Not lunch then, maybe a beer.

Down at the water, it was the lull between the morning rush of tour groups and the one pm rush for lunch, so he sat at an empty table and drank his beer and watched the wind rush over the top of the lake, ruffling the surface into tiny silver peaks. He squinted until all he could see was sparkle. It was peaceful, with only the infrequent grunts and comments of two old men drinking their espresso, and the chatter of two young mothers with babies sleeping in strollers, and since he couldn't understand a word the women said it was as though their words were background music, something like the flow of fountain water or the white noise rain tape he'd listened to in the plane on the way over.

White noise was a pleasant place to be, he thought, hazy and content after his beer. In a piazza full of white noise, a guy could relax and sit without thinking or analyzing his feelings. They were here in Italy on the advice of Julia's doctor. They were trying to have a child, and it wasn't looking good. It was his fault maybe, or maybe hers, or fault wasn't a word to be used here, the doctor at the clinic kept saying. But Julia wanted a kid, and she kept talking about it, and about her biological clock. She was older than him by two years. But what was the use of that, clock or no clock, things clicked or they didn't, and it looked like no click was the name of this game. And the whole spare bedroom thing in his parents' house hadn't helped of course, but still, they'd tried plenty. Walt spun his slippery beer glass in his fingers, and the waiter, without asking, brought him another and nodded companionably as he went back to converse with the two old guys.

So he drank down another and watched the small ferry that carried tourists back and forth from the mainland to this island garden. It chugged up to the dock and they cut the engine. Two men efficiently threw out the lines and pushed the metal ramp onto the pier and Walt got up, put the five euro note under his empty glass, and walked onto the boat.

No one asked for a ticket. He sat up front, where the wind would blow his hair, blow the cobwebs out as his old grandpa would have said. Beside him a family with two small kids, maybe twins, sat primly in the plastic seats, parents referencing their guidebooks. One of the kids elbowed the other and next thing he knew they were on the ground wrestling. The parents kind of ignored it. Would he ignore something like that, if he and Julia ever succeeded?

On his other side, an old lady and her even older mom sat, looking around with the same bright expectant gaze, as though they'd wanted to come here to the Italian Lakes forever and it was exactly meeting up with their raised expectations. He felt kind of happy, just looking at them. He didn't think a happy old age was in his future though, or Julia's. He rubbed his forehead and sat back in his seat, stretching out his legs and closing his eyes.

The boat didn't stay at the pier long. It loaded its dozen or so passengers, tossed off the ropes and away they went. He thought they'd head back to the main town of Stresa, where they'd come from this morning. He guessed he could wait for Julia there as easy as on the island itself. But instead the boat turned its nose north and chugged around a point into the wider section of the lake and it seemed they were headed somewhere new.

At the next stop, only two passengers got on. One was a single guy like himself who sat down behind him. Walt could feel the guy's gaze on the back of his neck. It made him want to brush it off or something. He got up and went down a few stairs into the indoor part of the boat. There was a bar here. Too bad he didn't have any cash. But when the waiter asked what he wanted, he said a birra and he drank it down in one long cold gulp when it came. When the guy was busy with someone else he pushed out into the back of the boat and found a single seat in the sun, sort of out of sight. He sat there and the boat went chugging on and they kept stopping at small ports and loading and unloading a few passengers at each and eventually the sun got lower and almost went behind the mountains and still they chugged on.

They reached a nice looking town with a fine substantial waterfront and there was lots of shouting. The crew tied up the boat and walked off, yanking off their jackets. They looked to be staying, so he got off too and wandered down the cobbled pedestrian walkway that followed the waterfront.

It was chilly, with a brisk wind, and when he looked up he saw they'd actually got a lot closer to the Alps; there they were, above, capped with snow just like all those magazine shots in travel ads he'd looked at back in NYC. Kind of surreal when an ad looked more like the Alp than the actual Alp did, but that was life nowadays. He always got philosophical after a beer, so he just kept on walking and ignored the mountains.

He passed several shops selling magazines and cigarettes, and a few cafes with empty tables. The signs, Walt realized, were in another language, something like German, and the restaurant food featured sausages and raclette. Somehow he had crossed a border; he was in Switzerland now. That was something. Had he gone through some checkpoint on the boat and not even noticed? He wasn't sure; he might have napped on that chair tipped against the wall in the sun. Probably did nap, maybe for an hour or so. Evidently they hadn't woken him up. Pretty casual about the border he guessed. He'd looked at a map of the lake briefly when Julia had shoved it in his lap but he hadn't noticed country boundaries, only the shape of the water and the intense blue color.

He strolled along the lakefront, watching the water turn turquoise and then violet in the setting sun and then suddenly it was blue-black and the sun had disappeared beyond the mountains and it was distinctly cold. People were hurrying past him, loaves of bread clutched in their hands along with briefcases. He was getting hungry; the beer was wearing off. He wondered if he could just push along with one of them and go home and eat the baguette with some nice slices of Swiss cheese and admire their rosy face children and sleep on their sofa. Probably not, he thought, noticing the thin bridges of their noses and the way they distinctly avoided meeting his eye. He tucked in his shirt and ran fingers through his black hair but there was no way he looked like one of them.

The gendarmes at the end of the walkway were standing in pairs, chatting, and only occasionally glancing at the crowd streaming from the waterfront up into the town in a controlled merge at the intersection. Lights were blinking on in the cafes and soon all these people would be eating their dinners. When he reached the police, half wondering if he should explain his predicament, the pair suddenly swung around and grasping his two elbows propelled him neatly into a waiting minivan and swung shut the doors.

It was dark inside; he seemed to be on some sort of seat. The minivan revved up its engine and swung around in a U-turn and was off up the bumpy street, its crazy two-tone European siren wailing. Walt swallowed, feeling nauseous. The beer had definitely worn off now. The dark swinging ride and the silence from the officers were making him nervous. If they'd just asked him, he could have explained, told them to call Julia, bring his passport, but throwing him in the van like this. All the stories about police in foreign countries rushed and tangled in his head. He was breathing too fast. But Christ, this was Switzerland. Though it was true, he hadn't paid for that beer. These guys would take that seriously, with their gleaming handcuffs dangling from their belts and handguns riding on their hips.

The van stopped; they shut off the siren. He watched them get out. But the back doors did not open. He was ready, with his explanations, but no one came. Did they go home to dinner or something? Christ sake Julia would be wondering where he was by now. That was good actually. Really good. But would she find someone to take her seriously, or would they think, just another missing husband?

Walt sat in the thick dark and tried not to think of the hours till dawn. He had to piss. He had to get out of here. When they let him out, would he be interrogated, like that poor immigrant looking guy on the train? Shaking fingers and pulling out his papers as fast as he could. I'm legal, the poor guy kept saying. His own hair was too black and his skin a shade too dark around here, Walt thought uneasily.

He didn't even have any papers to pull out. They were all in Julia's backpack. His passport, neatly rubber-banded with hers. He used to have papers, used to shuffle papers all day long, mountains of papers, but now when it mattered, he had none. Not that you could compare his situation with the mess that poor guy on the train was in. Still. It was awfully quiet now, outside the van. His own breathing was loud. He put his head in his hands and tried not to think at all.

An hour passed, or maybe two. Suddenly the van door screeched and cold fresh air rushed in and he felt like he could breathe again. "You are free to go," said one of the gendarmes slowly, in English.

"Hey, what was the problem? You guys had me locked up here for hours. If it was the beer, I can explain about that." The gendarme didn't even shrug, much less speak to him, just yanked him up onto the sidewalk, slammed the van door, got in and drove away.

Walt watched the van lights swaying up the street. What had that been about? At least in NY he knew what was going on, or thought he did. He hadn't known actually, if he were really honest. Hadn't known his best friend Craig had been playing with the accounts in some complicated game he couldn't even follow when they explained it to him. When they accused him of starting it. It had been Craig who'd started it, turned out, then lied and put the blame on him. He didn't think he would have done the same if the situation were reversed. But you never know what you'd do, really. And what did that matter now?

It appeared to be even later than he'd thought, and as Walt walked around, he saw the town was pretty much closed up for the night. He found a bar eventually, with a phone, and got the bartender to loan him a token to make the call, but Julia didn't pick up. That was strange. He had imagined her waiting anxiously by the phone, wondering where the hell he had gone, irritation turning to worry and then panic. Was she just sleeping soundly without him? Or worse? The bartender frowned when he returned, but put a small beer in front of him and let him stay there until two, when they closed up for the night.

Outside, it was cold. Summer, but sharp as late fall in New England here, as though he could see the white frost rimming pumpkin vines, with their twisty squirmy squiggles, like the fields he and Julia had seen in Vermont when they'd spent a weekend away. He turned up the collar of his thin jacket. He'd have to find a park bench, or a doorway, or something. He didn't have a lot of experience being homeless, though he'd seen plenty of it, back in NYC. He could do it, he thought, for one night. He thought of the king size bed in their hotel room and Julia, snuggled down into the sheets, the comforter tucked under her ears. The warm familiar smell of her. He sighed and started walking.

At the end of the cobble stone pedestrian area, he found a small park with a fountain, a lot of ducks with their heads tucked into a wing, and no one else. No one homeless here apparently. Or all chased away by those efficient gendarmes. Probably they'd leave him alone now though. Must have been a case of mistaken identity, or something. He should have kept quiet about the beer.

He sat down on a damp bench and listened to the water and the sound of leaves rustling across the concrete pavers. The fountain was made of three fat cherubs, spouting water from the top of their heads. They were fatter than any baby he'd seen, but cute. It was exhausting, all this trying, and seemed to drive him further away from Julia, never closer. It wasn't like he didn't want a kid. But they were fine as they were, weren't they? But they weren't. That was the bare truth. He wanted a kid too, really wanted two or three, but you didn't always get what you wanted. You had to take that, like a man. Life was like that. You had to just take it all.

He lay down on the bench, which was too short, and his legs hung uncomfortably over the end. He managed to squirm over onto his side, knees bent. Man, it was freezing. He watched the three cherubs out of half-closed eyes and tried not to shiver.

Morning light woke him, though really it was just a sliver of greyness, no beam of sunshine or anything like that. And maybe it wasn't the light at all, he was nearly frozen. He wondered if you could freeze to death in summer. Maybe you could in Switzerland. He sat up and rubbed his eyes.

"Thought you'd never wake up," said a voice behind him. He nearly jumped out of his skin. It was a girl, maybe fifteen, though it was hard to tell with the thick wool coat and piles of scarves she had looped around her neck.

"I need your help," she said.

He shook his head. "Sorry, I can't help you, I'm a stranger here myself, I've lost my papers, I've got no money." He stopped, realizing she'd spoken in English.

She was watching him, with very dark blue narrowed eyes. "I need you," she said, putting the accent on the you.

He thought there might be a hint of foreignness in her accent. Maybe eastern European or something, but so far, her English was pretty perfect, except she didn't seem to register what he'd said. "Sorry," he said louder, standing up. Wow, he was stiff and cold. He put up his empty palms. "Nothing, I've got nothing."

"Come with me," she said and grabbed one of his hands. She dragged him out of the park and down an alley between tall buildings. Around them he could hear the sounds of the town waking up, the clang of car doors, the shuffle of delivery truck doors. A grey kitten meowed and skirted through his feet. He pulled his hand from the girl's but she grabbed his elbow and hustled him along.

"Look," he said, "you need someone else." This was getting out of hand.

She gave him a look that he couldn't read and pulled him along. If only he'd had a coffee, he could think how to handle this. His brain was hardly ticking along at all. They reached another street and she opened a door at the end of the lane and pulled him into a kitchen. It was so warm he nearly cried. She thrust him down in an armchair by the hot stove and poured him a big bowl of hot coffee and milk from a pot bubbling on the gas burner. He took one sip then gulped the rest down. The hot latte poured down his throat, burning in a wonderful way, filling his stomach with heat. His forehead broke out in sweat and he blinked and looked around, feeling his head begin to clear.

The girl nodded as though satisfied. She refilled his bowl of coffee and said, "Now you wait," and left the room.

He should definitely not wait, he thought. He should get right up and walk out of here. But he couldn't make himself leave the smell of hot coffee and the heat flowing from the stove, holding him like iron filings to a magnet. The girl returned, with an older woman, grey hair in sausage-like bundles on her head. "Here," the older woman said and placed a rumpled cloth into his arms. He pushed it away.

The older woman shouted something, in some language he didn't know. The girl grabbed his two hands and peered into his eyes. "For you," she said.

Her eyes were intent and very very blue. He found himself taking the cloth she took from the old woman and pressed into his hands. It was moving, he realized, the white cloth rustling. Two round eyes peered up at him and widened as they met his gaze.

"You go now," said the girl. "It's best."

"What is this?" he said, and tried to push the baby back into the girl's arms.

"You want a child, don't you?"

"Yes, yes, of course I do," he said, but did he? They'd been trying of course, but this was something else entirely. And how did she know?

"Then here she is." The girl was looking impatient. She folded her arms over her chest.

"I can't take your child," he said slowly, thinking this was insane. What was going on? Why were foreign countries always so confusing? Where was Julia and what was going on?

"Not mine," said the girl and shrugged. "She is yours; take her, no one else will. We have tried and we can't keep her here any longer. She was meant for you. I knew as soon as I saw your face."

"What do you mean, no one else will?" There must be a mother somewhere, or a father, or an orphanage, or something. This was Europe. A civilized place with social services. Better than NY.

The girl pushed him, gently, but firmly, out the door and shut it behind him with a definite metallic snap of the lock.

"Wait! What the…" He hammered with one fist on the door, clutching the bundle of baby with the other, but the two women didn't answer.

He heard a clunk, like a heavy door slamming, and at the end of the street he saw the police minivan with its vivid red stripes.

"Go now," the girl shouted from inside. "Or they will come for us."

Walt turned and walked away from the police, the child in his arms, the cloth covering her nose. He stopped at the next intersection. He pushed the cloth aside with his thumb and the child stared up at him and her eyes widened again. She examined him, then blinked and gave him a wide lopsided grin.

He should turn right back and take her to those gendarmes. But what then? A lifetime in an orphanage, maybe adoption if she were lucky? Or would she be deported along with that girl and her grandma? Did they deport babies? He thought they did.

The baby squirmed in his arms and managed to catch his eye again. She smiled a huge full body smile and squealed. He found himself grinning back, like a crazy man.

He walked, slowly so he wouldn't stumble on the cobbles, thinking. Could he adopt her? He had no papers, she had no papers, but surely that could be resolved? What were lawyers for? Or maybe. He realized he was walking down the narrow street that led to the wharf. Could he just get back on the boat? Julia was very efficient. Hell, he could be very efficient, if there were a point to it. Of course he had no job these days. He had no money. But he could get a job, some job, he knew he could if he tried. The coffee raced through him and he felt expanded and suddenly full of energy, stretched and widened and awake. He strode down the narrow street, feeling his mouth crack into a smile.

He found himself back at the bar, where the sleepy cleaning woman let him use the phone again. When he called Julia, this time she picked up. "Where have you been all night? I've been frantic and then I had the most wonderful dream."

"I'm coming, I'm coming now, I'll tell you everything," he said, "buy me a ferry ticket online and I'll meet you, in any one of those Italian gardens you like. No, make it the one with the statue of the swimming dolphins."

He went out, the baby snuggled on his shoulder, to wait for the ferry. Looking like any tired father. Though now the gendarmes were nowhere to be seen. Looking out over the grey lake, he imagined a sea, its waters bright green and salty, its winds soft, and the god, he remembered now, was Dionysus, who bridges death with life.

ISOLA BELLA IN THE SPRING

The smell was unfamiliar and Cora couldn't tell if it was spicy or sweet, which was disorienting, like everything that had happened already that morning. She was wandering in a quiet, even neglected, corner of a famous formal garden where decaying leaves strayed over the brick edging the path. The smell could be a flower, she thought, or perhaps the leaf of a specific tree, but the scent seemed to permeate the air, not emanate from any one particular shrub. She knew she was fixated on the smell to avoid thinking about all the rest.

The smell was odd though and while it wasn't a stink, one wouldn't call it a fragrance either, which is what you'd expect floating on the breeze in a garden on the shore of an Italian Lake. Or Lago, as they said here. Nick used to like her scent, at least he said so often, and he'd bury his nose in the crook of her shoulder or along her neck and breathe her in. But she wasn't here to think about all of that.

She looked around with determination. Hot sun beat on her shoulders and on her head, her dark hair like a hot cap. She should have brought a hat. The cypress trees lining the path to her left were dark and appropriately mysterious. Every so often there was a clump of pansies plunked down between or in front of a tree, gold and cheerful, but the pansy leaves were wilted in the heat.

When she turned a corner, she saw a gardener kneeling by a clump of some sort of tall plumed grass. "Your pansies need water," she said.

He frowned at her and she supposed he didn't understand English, but then he said, with a strong British accent, "No they don't. Not really. And how would you know?"

That was certainly rude and nearly stopped her. "I know enough to know when a plant needs water," she said.

He laughed. "Perhaps you'd like a job."

"Perhaps I would."

"Ok then, help me get these in the ground."

It was a dare and she could never resist her older brother when he dared her so she dropped to her knees, grabbed the pink petunia this man handed her, knocked it out of its pot, dug a quick hole with one hand and dropped it in.

"Hey!" The gardener looked alarmed. Then he rocked back on his heels and laughed and handed her a spade. They worked companionably for an hour or more, not speaking, until nearly fifty plants were in the ground, a long row of ruffled pink and white blossoms. Cora repeated her thought about water.

"It will rain," he said, and when she looked up she thought

he could be right because crowding purple clouds were blowing in off the Alps, wind already darkening paths across the lake, and gusting at the top of the cypress hedge.

"Come on," he said, grabbing up the shovel and extra clay pots. She followed him along a gravel path, wind scattering leaves across her sandaled feet, and down some mossy stairs. They would be slippery when they got wet. They threaded along a narrow passage between two stone walls, dark with dripping water and unadorned.

He dropped the pots and tools beside a potting table and grabbed her hand. "Come on, run, we're in for it."

They ran and almost made it, but rain dumped down, drenching her in a moment and he pulled her into some sort of underground cellar strangely lined with seashells patterned like mosaics on the walls.

"It's the grotto," he said. "All these gardens have one."

Cora nodded, thinking back to her reading in the guidebook, and looked around. It was dark in here and empty. They were alone with the pearlescent gleam of the shells and the sound of rushing rain outside and she supposed they would make love now.

But the gardener, whose name she didn't even know yet, disappeared through a doorway deeper into the grotto. He didn't come back. After a while, she peered into the next room and saw there was a series of rooms, one after the other after the other. She could hear him clattering metal tools somewhere far along and the echo reverberated off the walls like the distant boom of waves.

She should wait by the door. The rain would stop and she could leave and all would be the same as it was. But that was what she couldn't stand. She had a sudden image of the hospital room with its accompanying smells and she clutched her wet sweater closer to her chest and ventured into the next room, toward the clattering sound.

Three days later hot sun beat on the back of her neck again and Cora was still on Isola Bella, though she should have gone on to Milan and taken the fast train down to Florence by now. She had a single room at a cheap pensione right in Stresa and she'd taken the ferry over to Isola Bella each morning around nine. She'd found the gardener and worked alongside him. He'd looked at her the first morning, his grey eyes puzzled, but he'd shrugged and hadn't asked her a single question. Which suited her fine.

Her phone beeped so she dug it out of her pocket. The beep turned out to be a signal she'd run out of charge. She stared at the dark screen. Now she'd have no idea if Nick had tried to get her or not. A hot wind stirred the hair at her neck and she glanced out at the lake, rippled with waves. A clunk and the sound of laughter floated up from the dock, the first load of tourists for the day.

She dropped the phone into a trash can and covered it with a heaping armful of drooping weeds. That felt decisive. It wasn't that Nick deserved it. He'd tried so hard to be kind. But it all hung there in the air, always between them. It just didn't seem possible to resume the normal rhythm of their normal days. What a betrayal that would be. But she didn't kid herself that just walking away was any better.

Everything has its season. She'd known that of course, but the gardener, whose name was Tony, kept repeating it. Plants had different life spans, it seemed, just like people.

"Some live for eighty years and some for two," said Tony. His real name was Antonio and he was a graduate student in philosophy at one of the British universities but he lived in a suburb outside Milan. He came to the garden each morning on the train and jogged down the hill to the granite pier where a friend of his tied a power boat. They'd rev the double engines and zoom off to Isola Bella. Tony would leap onto the dock and his friend would wave before heading out to scoop up tourists in too much of a hurry to wait for the regular ferry.

After three weeks working as an unpaid gardener's assistant, Cora's back no longer ached and her calves were tanned and her ankles spotted with bug bites. She'd planted thousands of pansies and daisies in long straight rows. Today, for the first time, Tony was going to let her design and plant six of the giant terra cotta pots. She gazed at the array of small flowers in tiny pots stretching out in front of the greenhouse, like watercolors lined up ready for a painter's brush.

"Don't forget the vertical," said Tony.

"I'm not likely to," she answered. He always seemed to know it all. And he was always laughing.

She spent the whole morning experimenting and decided in the end on three plants for each pot. Artemisia with silver leaves hanging out and trailing in the breezes, gentian with its gold-centered sprays of tiny blue flowers, and a tall spiky white lily with multiple buds in the center, towering in a protective way, she thought, over the frailer flowers.

"Nice," Tony said as he passed by, his arms loaded down with earth-encrusted shovels, "but you'll have to separate out the lilies, their roots suck all the water from the others."

It took her well into the night to put the lilies in an inner pot within the larger, and to complete her regular work for the day. But she finished shoveling and weeding and carting fertilizer in time to set the pots out so Tony would see them first thing in the morning.

She collapsed on the narrow bed in the pensione and gazed at the cracked green wall and imagined more and larger and wilder projects. Sticky leaves and spiky succulents and giant palms invaded her dreams. In the morning, not feeling especially rested, still she was up early and gulped her espresso and when she saw her pots arrayed along the western walkway, the flowers still spangled with dew, she felt a small thrill. How wonderful, to feel something.

But later, as she raked leaves from under the cypress, she realized she'd picked lilies because that's what everyone had sent, and in a moment she was right back where she'd started. It wasn't going to be possible to forget. She leaned on her rake, her fingers trembling, her stomach tight. She needed to learn from the plants, feel their contentment, their lack of striving, their taking whatever came their way and still pushing out new shoots, but she wasn't a plant, who was she kidding.

She gazed out past the terraced garden at the silvery wash of water. She wasn't Italian either and while Antonio seemed mildly interested in her at times, he had a much younger girlfriend and stuck her on the back of his motorcycle to zoom around the town. She pinched the extra skin at her waist.

One afternoon, after she started to get paid for her work, Cora came across Tony reading the newspaper, his brows drawn together in a way she'd never seen. "The comics can't be that sad," she said, attempting a joke. It flopped, because he looked up at her, strain tightening his mouth and he threw the paper down and walked off. Later, he was his usual loud and laughing self and she wondered how she'd annoyed or bothered him somehow. After dinner, she went back in the dusk of evening and picked the soggy newspaper out from the trash and looked at the headlines. One about a fire in an apartment building in Venice, one about a bombing in Afghanistan, another about banking corruption in Rome. An endless array of problems to be sad about. Which one had he been reading? She tossed the paper away, angry at herself. What did she care anyway, about him, about anything? That tiny threads of curiosity were beginning to sprout again made her despair. Wasn't it possible to care deeply about something, about someone, and never forget?

The smell of the children's hospital had been the same each day when she'd walked in. It hit her nose and clogged her throat and made her eyes water. It was disinfectant, stamping out germs, those that could be stamped out. The others, that couldn't, had to be ignored. They swabbed Eliza's floor twice a day, but what use was that? She and Eliza would stop their game of checkers or their reading of fairy tales and wait, hushed, as though disinfecting were a religious ritual and they hoped for some positive outcome.

She liked the dirt in this garden, Isola Bella. Liked the rings of earth under her fingernails and the brown stains on the knees of her jeans. She only rinsed her fingers at the end of each day and never tried to wash it all off.

Antonio kept a pistol in his locker. Cora saw it hanging from a thick leather belt when she jostled close to him one evening after they'd set out three hundred new roses of three different varieties. "Why do you have that? Can I hold it?" she asked.

"Sure, why not," he said, but he didn't laugh.

She took it eagerly and hefted it in her palm. "It feels good," she said.

He took it from her and clicked shut the combination lock on his locker. "Not really," he said.

She followed him out through the wrought iron gate and up the moss covered granite stairs. "But why do you have it, are you with the police or something?" She looked around but there was nothing to see, only rows of orange trees in the orange light of sunset and a few late tourists winding off the ferry down below, their voices shrill.

"No," he said. "Not the police."

"Perhaps you're a spy then." She laughed.

He grabbed a pot from a shelf at the turn of the stairs and yanked out the wilting marigold and replaced the pot, empty, on the shelf. "What would you know about that?" he said, his voice too loud. "Have I ever asked you what you're doing, planting flowers here at Isola Bella?" He pointed to her wedding ring. "Let well enough be," he said and went into the greenhouse, with its tables lined with marigolds, hundreds of marigolds, in small pots.

He made her feel ashamed and that made her angry. She abandoned the marigolds and him and went down the stairs to the far shore of the island, away from the tourists and the market stalls and the mainland. She sat by the water, grey and slapping endlessly against the rock walls. Why couldn't she live like a perch or a rose or a stone, without a past or future? Why was it so great to be a person?

She listened to the water slapping until the wind chilled her and the dark descended. When she got back to the greenhouse the marigolds were all gone, and all the tiny pots were stowed away.

"Come on," said Antonio, coming up silently behind her, making her start. "Let's get a drink." He didn't sound mad anymore. They didn't head off island, as she thought they would. Instead, he returned to the grotto. She followed him past the shell chamber, through several dark rooms, until they reached a small room with a wood table. It was cold.

Tony lit a candle. "Here," he said and gave her his jacket. He pulled a bottle of prosecco from behind a chest and she wondered if he planned this or he did it often and whether there was one bottle back there or a dozen. They drank, passing the bottle back and forth between them, sitting on an uncomfortable bench covered in snail shells in a floral pattern, saying nothing. The wine was fizzy and too warm, way sweeter than she liked. She knew he was going to tell her something; this was the prelude. She wasn't sure she wanted to hear. Why did she have to hear another story? Didn't she have her own? She took a swig of the wine, got up and went out through the various chambers, leaving him.

Two days later, when she opened her locker in the morning, there was her cell phone, clean and shining, on the shelf. She picked it up and examined it. It still needed a charge, but the phone felt warm on her palm, like Nick felt when he took her hand in his. She wondered what he'd been doing these nine weeks and if he thought she was dead too. She put the phone back on the shelf and shut the locker door.

"You should call him," said Tony the next day while they weeded around the purple and white orchids.

"Call who," she said.

"There is someone."

"Was," she said.

"Is," he insisted.

She looked over at him, studying the orchid roots and trailing stems, searching for aphids, and realized she hadn't heard him laugh in days. "Hey, you're all right, aren't you?" she said.

"Of course," he said. "Whatever."

The next afternoon, after they watered the giant pots of limes and tied up the stray branches on the wisteria, she came across him studying the newspaper again. He didn't look at her. "I guess I'll go back there," he said.

"Back where?" She sat down on the bench opposite him.

He shrugged. "Afghanistan."

"Were you a soldier? Is that why you have the gun?"

"Am. I deserted. Left. Fled."

She shifted on the rough wood seat. "Was it so awful?"

He was quiet for a long time. "Yes," he said finally.

"Why go back then? They'll never find you here. You can make a new life. You've made one already."

He looked at her.

"Almost," she said.

He shrugged, staring at a hole in his pants over his knee and poking at it with his index finger. "There was a kid. I killed his father. Had to, he would have killed me. But the kid's face."

"That's awful," Cora said carefully. "But, what good would it do to go back? Wouldn't it just be more, of that?"

"I could find him."

"The kid? How? In a war? Would he even want to come with you? I mean, doesn't he hate you?" She swallowed. That hadn't come out right.

"I don't know. Probably. But maybe not. And who knows what his life is like now, if he's even alive? What if he has no one? He was just a kid, eight maybe or nine. But who knows if it would even be good to bring him here, away from his own culture and all, you know? I mean, I don't even know if he had anyone, any family."

Cora nodded and they went back to weeding but now her mind was jumping around and wouldn't be calmed by the smell of earth or the feel of leaves in her fingers. Antonio had turned into another person entirely, not just some gardener, but a person with a past and some uncertain sort of future.

She didn't want him to have a past or future; she didn't want them herself.

She looked out over the potted orange trees, arranged in a symmetrical pattern on a terrace high above the silvery lake. She stood up and surveyed it all, the palm trees, the granite statues, the lake, and the Alps, wiping her palms together. Wind tossed her hair across her face and she closed her eyes and inhaled the smell of warmed earth and she rested, just for a moment, hot sun on her cheeks and forehead, burning.

THE PALM GARDEN IN WINTER

Entering the third palm garden in a single week, Jesse was already used to the caress of humid air on her cold cheeks. But this garden, she decided, might be the best of all. Date palms rose to the glass ceiling and beyond the glass grey clouds misted the surface and caused a lovely dim light to shimmer over all the plants. There was no glare here. She appreciated that, after the crazy trip, safari really to the pyramids of Giza, trailing after Jim. Always trailing. He was ahead of her right now – he'd shoved open the door and was holding it for her, polite, patient, talking with the guide and referencing his museum brochure with appropriate seriousness.

Jesse walked in the opposite direction, ignoring Jim's puzzled look, strolling the circular path that flowed around the palms. She examined the bark of each tree, and then each leafy plant, lush and green and healthy, as though she cared or could possibly tell one from another. One burst of sticky fat leaves had a single stalk topped with a lily-like white blossom and exuded a fragrance which floated on the humid air, smelling sweet and somewhat sharp, like a cat.

She could hear Jim murmur and the guide answer. She could see the middle-aged Danish ladies sipping chocolate at the café on the balcony overlooking the palms; she could see a single woman, sitting very straight and all alone, her blonde hair in a messy bun at the exact top of her head. The woman looked down as she passed and Jesse wondered what she saw. A pale woman in a green coat with dark red hair hanging rather tangled down her back, alone as well. Did she inspire curiosity? She'd always hoped to look, not glamorous, but at least slightly mysterious.

It didn't seem she'd achieved it though. The woman with the bun returned to staring at her menu. Then suddenly she looked up and glared right at her. Startled, Jesse moved on.

She examined a marble statue of a cupid, an abundance of fat thighs and drapery swirls, water flowing from a discreet fountain at the top of his tossed-curls head, and white blossoms, cyclamens according to the helpful plaque, enveloping an artificial pool of black water. Jesse studied the statue and the plants and the sign; she crouched down and rubbed a bit of the dark earth between her fingers.

When she looked back, the woman with the blonde bun was still staring at her, a frown drawing her dark brows close together. Jesse felt her chest shrink under her coat and she turned away quickly and climbed a set of oversized stairs and entered a hall, or rather something like the word forum came to mind. Glancing back, she saw the woman stand up. Flustered, wondering what she'd done to call attention to herself, or whether she'd done something very wrong, Jesse hurried through the long hall, her boot heels clunking on the marble floor, past the Roman statues, through the glass and steel double doors, into the modern wing of the museum. Jim would be here somewhere. He appreciated art that required thought.

She darted down a set of stairs and entered a room labeled Art of the Mediterranean. It was dim and chock full of statues and empty of people. She took a long deep breath. She was being ridiculous. Jim would be angry when he discovered she'd gone on ahead of him. Her role, clearly defined, was to trail behind. She waited for a few minutes, in the consoling dim light, enjoying the quiet, then she strolled on, threading her way between the many statues, with their graceful arms, flowing drapery, and chopped off fingers.

There seemed to be no guards in this part of the museum, which was rather pleasant. No yawning official watching her encounter the art. They always made her self-conscious, though she knew they were just desperately bored and anything in motion was liable to draw their eyes.

She passed through a wide doorway and entered a second long rectangle of a room, painted deep moss green and here were more statues, lots of them, arms pointing this way and that, like the winter limbs of a slender tree, a forest of trees. She touched the white marble of one arm and ran her forefinger down a fold of cloth over a powerful thigh, because in the absence of guards, she could. The marble was cool and smooth. She thought of Jim's unexpectedly hairy thighs and pushed the image away.

No other visitors were around so she floated through a string of rooms, reading the inscriptions when there was an English translation and puzzling over the Danish when there was not. The museum had been built to house the art collection of a beer brewer, she read in her brochure. She paused to think about that. This brewer had certainly loved art. How amazing to acquire an actual Roman statue. How did you even do that? Even back then, a century ago or more, there must have been difficulties. Did he go on scouting trips himself or simply send an agent? Why did this Danish brewer have such an affinity for Romans and Rome? She might have liked him, but perhaps not. Should this art be here in this cold northern country, or did it belong back in Italy? She wasn't sure. The palm garden in the central courtyard was certainly nice.

She fingered the fat gold band on her left hand, lit by a pattern of tiny diamonds. The ring was heavy and expensive and traditional, exactly what Jim would like and he'd put it on her finger four months ago, in the Palm House at Kew, outside London, as they stood under a frighteningly healthy tree with long dangling vines which concluded in oval fruits which swung in the breeze, nearly clunking them on the head. Jesse had found herself pondering the fruits and their weird sexual roles rather than listening to Jim's speech which was too bad because after she wondered if it had truly been convincing and she wondered also exactly what she'd agreed to.

It was lovely, so calm and quiet in these subterranean galleries. The walls were newly painted alternating white or mossy green, the floors grey marble, and the statues displayed in congenial groupings, much closer and more crowded than in most museums she'd been to. More like the statues were actual people, gathered to converse or have a cocktail. She liked it, she decided, but she knew already that Jim would be provoked into a discussion of minimalism and the virtue of the sparse.

Somewhere, a metal door slammed, and the sound echoed through the various chambers. Jesse glanced at her watch. Four pm. Didn't the museum close at five? Dismayed, she looked ahead into the next room, to all the rooms she didn't have time to see, but she'd best turn around and go back.

She threaded back though the rooms she'd already toured; she'd been through three or maybe four she thought but as she walked she realized it was more like seven or eight.

Another door slammed, far ahead, and the boom echoed among the statues. She walked faster, a little alarmed now, and reached the entryway. It was sealed off with a thick plywood door with galvanized iron hinges. She pushed at it. It was definitely shut tight and already locked. She felt a surge of panic but shook her head and tried to laugh.

She'd just have to go out a different door. No doubt they closed off some doors to herd visitors out the right way at closing time. Not that there were many visitors here. She walked back through the necklace of rooms, ignoring the outstretched arms and noseless faces of the statues. She reached the room she'd been in before and went on through. Another room, empty of live people. Where were all the people who loved ancient art? She hurried through and reached a wide doorway and walked out into a huge hall. For a relieved moment she thought it was the forum she'd come through at the start, but then she realized the color was wrong. This marble was a fleshy pink and covered the walls and floor. The ceiling was high and painted with figures that she could only partly see in the dim light. As she gazed upward the lights in the one chandelier at the room's center flicked on and off, twice.

She rushed to the other end of the hall, slipping once on the marble tiles but catching herself, but there was no doorway here; she could see no way in or out. She turned back and just as she faced the huge hall the lights flickered again and then went out. "Hey," she called and ran a few steps, but it was pitch dark and she stopped, her face enveloped in thick air smelling of stone and old dust. She thought, what is Jim doing? She imagined him, earnestly discussing some point of art history with the guide, never realizing she'd left his side, much less become lost and locked in. For a moment, she wanted to feel his firm thigh crowding next to hers, like he always did on a bus seat or at the theatre, taking up his seat and also some of hers.

Her eyes grew accustomed to the dark and she could just see enough to edge her way along the wall, back toward the doorway, she hoped. It was so very dark.

There was an unexpected smell when she re-entered the statue rooms. Almost like frying sausage and that was pretty unlikely. She was hallucinating already, she thought with gloom. And that was so overwrought she had to laugh.

It was very dark, almost like feeling her way through thick velvet rather than air; her chest hurt and she had to remember to slow her breathing. A panic attack was not what she needed now. She stopped and made herself exhale longer than she inhaled, and finally her heart slowed down and her diaphragm relaxed and she blinked a few times, trying to see. She looked around, though she could see little. Only vague ghostly marble arms, pointing in every direction, none signaling which way was out.

Then she heard a laugh. It was long and low and certainly a woman. She took a step toward the laugh and blundered into a statue, which luckily seemed to be bolted onto its pedestal. What if she had toppled a priceless goddess or some Roman orator's head? It was quiet again and then she heard a distant clatter and a slam and a definite sound, like a deadbolt, a large and powerful deadbolt, locking into place. "Hey!" she called out and her voice echoed back to her. "Hey," she said, but softly this time, cowed by the echoes and the feeling that all the statues and maybe someone else was listening.

There was silence and dark. And then a voice spoke, so close behind her, she started and slammed her wrist into a pedestal. She stifled a groan. The voice spoke again. "Who are you, what are you doing here?" a man said, in a heavy accent that she couldn't place.

"Well, who are you?" she said and hoped that sounded assertive enough.

The man was silent a moment and then laughed. "I'm no one," he said, "and I'm not here."

Despite the laugh, the last part sounded menacing. Jesse took a step back, still clutching her wrist, which ached and now she realized she was bleeding down her fingers and onto the floor. This man, she realized, wasn't a museum employee. She took another step back.

The man reached out then, and grabbed her wrist. She sucked in a breath.

"What is wrong, are you injured?"

This seemed an odd thing for an antiquities thief or whatever he was to ask her. He flipped her wrist over and his fingers pressed probing and flexing. "It's a sprain, not broken," he said calmly, "but you must be bandaged up. Come."

This was all so surreal, Jesse didn't think of disobeying. She trailed along beside him as he guided her with a light touch at her shoulder, down through the line of statues and through some doors and down some dark stairs and through more doors and into a small chamber, with one tiny window set way up high and barred with metal. The smell of sausages was strong and spicy and her stomach rumbled.

The open window let in some light. It was just growing dusk outside; a faint puff of mist blew in and she smelled the damp winter streets. From a dark corner behind a sheet hung from the ceiling pipes a woman with dark brows peered out. She spoke to the man, quickly, urgent, in some language that sounded either Eastern European or Middle Eastern or something, Jesse couldn't be sure.

"Sit," said the woman suddenly, in English. "She will faint," she said to the man.

He pushed her down onto a stool and shoved her head down between her knees and Jesse felt the sick cloudiness fade and she stayed down, breathing, glad to be in the dim light and out of the thick smothering dark.

"I'm ok," she said, "just claustrophobic I guess."

The woman stared at her with intent eyes of some light color. Jesse wasn't sure she understood and she tried again. "The dark, the closed in."

The woman nodded then. "Yes, it is bad, to be sealed in. Rest." She turned back to the man and they resumed their murmured conversation.

Jesse leaned back, her head against the concrete wall. There was a whimper and the woman went behind the curtain and came back with a smiling baby, maybe six months old, with curling dark hair on the top of its head. She held the child up to be admired so Jesse, who was frightened of children, smiled as wide as she could and said, "Beautiful."

Her mind was shifting back into gear. This was all so extremely odd. Why were these people here, in the basement of the museum, and with a baby? What was going on? The man had pulled out a well-stocked first aid kit with a red crescent on the top right corner and he was bandaging her wrist, expertly bandaging it as much as she could tell. She tried to sit up straighter.

He put her bandaged arm down on her lap and said, "It will be fine in one week, you should let it rest. And you must eat something sweet when you leave here and drink some water. You will feel strong again, like yourself."

Jesse looked into his dark eyes and he turned away from her and replaced the unused bandage and tape in the medical kit and closed the cover. Her head was thrumming with the start of a first class aching. Had she ever felt strong, she wondered, and then immediately she felt ashamed. What did she have to complain of? A somewhat injured wrist was nothing.

She remembered Jim then. He would be searching for her by now. "I must go," she said and stood up.

"Rest some more," said the woman, jiggling the baby on her knee, who stared at her and smiled again.

She found herself smiling back. "But I can't stay; it will be dangerous, for you. Someone is looking for me," she said. Just then there was a loud scraping noise somewhere back in the hall and the sound of excited voices.

The woman clutched the baby who began to cry. "Shush," she whispered and took the child behind the curtain.

"Thank you," said Jesse to the man, who watched her get to her feet, his face closed and tense. He nodded, picked up his kit, and slipped behind the curtain too.

Jesse edged her way out of the room and floundered back through the statues toward the voices, bumping into one and another. When she got closer, she called out to them. "I'm here, here. Jim, is that you?"

A flashlight beam landed on her chest as though she were a target. She wanted to duck behind a statue but she didn't, she walked out into the stream of light, one arm over her head like some sort of criminal, the other behind her back. "I'm here, it's me. I got locked in. I got lost," she said.

Jim grasped her arm. She wanted to gasp but she stifled the sound in her mouth and tugged her sleeve down over the bandage. "I'm fine, it's fine now. I'm so sorry," she said to the guard who looked at her with a sour face. "So foolish of me. I lost track of the time. Can we go up please, into the light?"

The guard swung his flashlight around in a wide circle, landing on each of the statues with their blank eyes and noseless faces, picking out the fingers and laurel wreaths and draped gowns of stone. It was silent and dark outside the light, heavy and waiting. "Thought I heard something," said the guard.

"Please," said Jesse, "I'm so tired. And I was frightened being locked in like that."

Jim and the guard looked at her with identical annoyed expressions. But they turned and escorted her out, one on each side.

They passed through darkened rooms and locked doors and out onto the street. The guard locked the door behind them. Mist swirled around their boots.

As they walked down the street, crowded with cyclists and walkers heading home from work, Jesse wondered where the family came from and where they were headed. She wished there had been time to ask. Because of her blunder, they would feel they must move on and the museum basement must be better than so many other places. She hoped she hadn't endangered them too much. She wondered when they would go. She wanted to return the next morning but knew she better not. She thought about the suspicious eyes of the guard and the blank eyes of all the statues, watching in the darkened rooms. She thought about the smile of the baby. She resisted turning to look back one more time, though she wanted to see the man's face as he crouched over his child and wife, enveloping them in his careful arms and trying to keep them safe.

A TENDRIL OF IVY

A tendril of ivy reaches across the statue's face, so that Cupid looks surprised and a little delighted. Perhaps imagining that Psyche herself stands behind him, her tentative fingers reaching out, stroking his cheek. He's frozen, unable to turn and see her standing there, amazed at her own temerity. Also, he'll never realize it was just ivy, wayward, touching him so tenderly. He'll never know he is alone.

Aiden wrinkled his nose at his own ridiculous fancy. Still, the statue makes him sad, so that he wants to turn away. Instead, he put a shoulder to the rusty gate, ignoring what it might do to his expensive suit. It creaked open a few inches, just enough to let him shove through.

He balanced on a mossy slab of granite inside the enclosed fence, so dense with ivy, it's impossible to see in or impossible for him now to see out. A sign says "Private Property" in block English letters, which is odd in itself, but it was written so long ago that it's faded and tipped sideways, and even though he's a lawyer back in real life, he thinks it doesn't matter anymore.

Because he wants to go on. That he's a curious person is a new discovery, only realized three days after his fortieth birthday, and he's been pondering it, considering going with it, ever since Samantha left.

He bundles that thought away by stepping forward. The grass is thick and grows in tufts that threaten to trip him up but he follows a path that runs along an allee of pleached pear trees. There are lichened stepping stones, toppled and uneven, more trouble than walking off the path through the grass, but the grass is so tall, draped with seed pods dripping in the damp morning, so he sticks to the stones. He passes an old foundation. Lovely granite piled in precise walls covered in amber lichen and emerald moss and wet; a spring bubbles up and creates a puddle that was probably once a bathing pool. Maybe ancient Romans lingered here once. He stands, gazing at the pool, musing. It's not very sunny and not an auspicious place but perhaps the cedars were shorter then and the walkway correspondingly dry and bright, the ivy less invasive and a view of blue sparkling lake could have been apparent from a second floor. Today, it's a chilly morning and the lake, if he could see it, would be choppy, and maybe it was always chilly here and dismal and sad. Aiden sits down on a pile of granite blocks and thinks: I bring sad with me wherever I go. There's little more to be said, so after a while he gets up and walks on.

There's less of a path here and the trees grow taller. He's left the tended part of the abandoned estate and entered the cultivated "wilderness" where one could dream about another life, an alternative to the one he is currently living. Sure, he thinks, even

Romans did that. Not the stoical ones, but the rest. The grass is high as his chest and he's wading through it, like wading through the lake or an ocean bay. The footing is dicey. He thinks he might sprain an ankle and as soon as he thinks it he slips on a slanted rock and falls over, disappearing into the tall wet grass.

When he tries to stand up, his ankle stabs and burns. He sits back down and notices it's turning from mist to an actual sprinkle of rain. He tips his face up to the grey sky and closes his eyes and sighs. A drop of water runs off his hair and trails its way down his neck. He's going to have to trudge back, dragging his painful ankle, and find a clinic in the town to bandage him up, but right now he's just going to avoid all that and sit.

A finger on the back of his neck startles him. He jumps up and pain shoots up his calf. A girl, no more than ten or twelve, is standing there in a thin cotton dress getting wet and transparent. He averts his eyes and she laughs. "You should come with me," she says. Her voice is low and melodious with some language he doesn't know how to speak. He knows he should do nothing of the kind but he finds himself limping after her, her white dress flashing in the greyness of soft falling rain.

She turns off into a stand of cedars and suddenly they're on a tended path between aromatic trees, maybe cypress or eucalyptus or something like that. Green seed pods crunch underfoot. She walks swiftly and he has trouble to follow. He thinks: she can bandage up my ankle, though she doesn't look much like a nurse. She turns to her right, disappearing suddenly, and he almost panics, but she waits for him, laughing, and beckons. He follows her and finds a small house, a hut really or a cottage to his eyes, its roof all thatched with green boughs so it blends in and he might have walked right on by. He hesitates a moment, because it all seems strange like one of those fairy stories his aunt used to read to him, but then he steps over the doorway into the warmness and the dark.

The girl laughs again and lights a lantern and bustles up the fire in the tiny hearth to a full blaze. They are alone. She gestures to a wood chair and he sits, his ankle throbbing. She shuts the outside door. Rain thrums on the thatch and some dribbles into the room. He watches a tiny puddle form in one corner. The floor is earth and smells of gardens and maybe of worms. He thinks of times that he's been in danger. Like that time on the coast path with Samantha when they got too high and far out on a cliff and had to turn around and edge their way downward clinging to the rocks. And that other time, he and Sam heading to Marseilles on a backroad past midnight, the rented car coughing and jerking along the winding cliffs in the dark, and Sam turning up the music and laughing. And that time in high school, before he ever knew Sam, with a crowd of boys in the back seat of his father's car egging him on so he got in a race with one of the seniors from shop class. He'd thought he'd never seek out danger again. But Sam had loved it, the thrill made her laugh and sing. But why think of danger at all in this warm dim place, his ankle stretched out by the blaze?

The air feels thick and almost hard to breathe. The fire is lovely but strangely streaked with green and blue. Perhaps this girl means to fix his leg or offer him a coffee or maybe her mother is going to appear. In the old stories, old women are the danger. The rain thrums down harder; they are enveloped. He couldn't leave, even if he wanted to.

The girl sits down opposite him and now he sees she's older than he thought. In fact, there are tiny lines crinkling out from the corners of her eyes and tiny drops of rainwater dribble from her ear down her neck where they disappear into the white cloth of her dress. She looks straight at him and he sees her eyes are grey or maybe greenish and she has black brows and translucent skin, also very white.

They sit in silence. He wonders how to begin. He wonders if he doesn't understand. He wonders why he doesn't just get up and walk out.

The girl pulls something from her dress pocket, something heavy, and he sees it's a chunk of marble, carved into a tiny delicate head, curls trailing around a long neck and down over a shoulder. The nose is smashed and one side of the head is missing a piece.

The girl holds the head out on two outstretched palms and when he reaches for it she laughs and snatches it away and returns it to her pocket. She says something then, a long complicated sentence in some Italian dialect way beyond his abilities, and when he doesn't answer she rakes apart the fire, snuffs the lantern, and walks out the door. He waits for her to return, but she doesn't, so after a while he opens the door, and finds that the rain has ceased and the cedars are steaming and the gnats have come out and the girl, she's gone.

Aiden limps back down the path. It seems to have grown colder and darker though it must be only two or three in the afternoon. The clouds are so low they meet the mist and shroud the top and trunks of the cedars and the smell of wood is sharp in the damp air. He should retrace his steps, find the rusty gate; it's getting late. He has a train to catch, back to Milan.

But where did the girl go? Was she offering to sell the statue to him? Was she a girl at all, or a woman? Was she even there, or something he imagined? He stops walking and stands in the path, the air so damp that oval drops are forming on his shirt front and sliding down his neck. He feels: I'd love to possess a piece of that lovely marble Diana or Psyche. It feels important. Like it might help. He glances at his palm, slick with rain and empty. The tiny statue, her shoulder had looked just like Sam's, the way she'd turn back to say something to him, something more, and smile. And now she'd gone where he couldn't hear what she was saying, he couldn't follow. He didn't feel any of those things people said, like she was hovering or protecting or watching. Ghost or guardian angel. She was gone, just gone. The air was empty. He was here in the northern lakes of Italy instead of home on the streets of Boston where he probably belonged, only he'd thought the air might feel less empty here.

He edged down the path, wincing, until he emerged from the overbearing trees into a wide clearing and finally he could breathe. A breeze stroked the tops of the tall grasses and set them swaying. In the center of the field, standing all alone, rose an ungainly house of three stories, with high windows, some with broken panes and some shuttered tight.

Aiden walked in closer and saw the three stories were all different styles, as though built in consecutive centuries, but the overall effect wasn't beauty. The house was dilapidated, the blue door paint peeling, the elaborate carved masonry crumbling. On the third floor one shutter suddenly flapped open and rapped against the walls.

He couldn't stop now. He tested the wooden steps and pushed

at the wooden door. It had been locked once, but the wood around the lock had rotted and he shoved the door open. Inside he heard the scrabbling of rats running away or maybe of bats flitting in the high ceilings. It was so dark he couldn't see what was up there.

Outside, he heard a crack of thunder and silver rain streamed down again. His leg aching, he sat on an empty crate just inside the threshold and watched water pour down the porch pillars, sliding over the carved garlands of flowers and down the fluted sides.

"You can't be here," said a voice in accented English. Aiden jumped up, nearly falling when his leg stabbed and buckled. He stared at a stocky man in dark clothing.

"I can't exactly go," he said, pointing to his ankle, which had swollen up and was beginning to purple where his pants were rolled up. The man frowned and snapped a finger. Two younger men with wet hair slicked back from their foreheads so they almost seemed like twins emerged from the shadows under the tall twisting staircase and one held his shoulders while the other bound his wrists behind his back.

"Sit there, since you want to," said the stocky man and they left him lying in the center of the dusty floor.

Aiden imagined gangs and drugs and Mafia tales. He found he was very hungry and he imagined sandwiches of salami and produce, like tomatoes warm from the sun and green peppers drenched in olive oil and pepper. He was thirsty and he thought of Chianti and Brunello and then of just spring water, cold and full of bubbles. The dim room creaked and darkened and finally it was so dark he could see nothing, however he strained his eyes. His ankle ached. He thought, they would have killed me already if they meant to, and tried to feel comfort, and finally he slept.

When Aiden opened his eyes, he could see morning had come. He woke up pleased from some pleasant forgotten dream, but when he looked up at the dim ceiling and realized his arms throbbed from being tied, he remembered where he was.

The front door had been shut and the house felt quiet and empty. He managed to sit up and then get to his feet. He decided to take a look around. There was a formal dining room with cobwebs right out of Dickens, an immense golden drawing room or such for dancing, a moldy library of empty shelves and discarded torn books strewn over the floor, and an empty kitchen, cold and silent and smelling of mildew or maybe mouse. There were footprints made by men's boots on the dusty floors. In the last room, there was a bed, still rumpled, where someone had been sleeping. Someone small and light. He moved closer, dragging his injured leg.

He stared at the sheets and imagined he smelled the rain and dirt scent of the girl. On the night table was a knife. He used it to shred the cord binding his wrists, cutting himself twice. There was a tall clear decanter full of water. He emptied it, gulping and spilling, and sighed and then he saw, placed behind a vase filled with fern fronds, the marble head with its blank eyes. He rubbed the blood from his fingers and picked up the statue and examined her lovely shoulder and long neck and straight nose, so unlike Sam's and yet. The tiny statue's eyes were gazing on nothing or everything perhaps, eternity even. She could see Sam; he could believe that.

He reached in his pocket and pulled out his wallet, which the slick-backed youths had ignored, and he placed a hundred dollar bill under the glass decanter. But that didn't feel right. He took the money and shoved it back in his pocket. He could give it to that homeless woman he'd seen wrapped in a pink blanket near the train tracks.

He limped through the house, ignoring the throbbing in his ankle, but the girl was not there, no one was there, not in any of the empty echoing rooms. No one appeared as he crossed the high grassy meadow or as he dragged his foot down the long uneven path. He stopped often and looked for the girl, hoping, but she was gone; they were gone, all of them, somewhere.

When he left the garden, shutting the rusty gate behind him, there was nothing to do but trudge up the long hill to the clinic to get his ankle bandaged. Fingering the marble head in his pocket, thinking of Psyche on the eternal hunt for love, and missing Sam.

ACKNOWLEDGMENTS

First, to Morgan and Hannah, thank you for inviting me to stay with you in Milan, letting me spend time in the gardens and by the lakes of Northern Italy, and also spend precious time with you. These stories wouldn't exist without you!

Thank you also to the wonderful writer teachers whose workshops taught me so much about the short story, especially to Stacey Swann, Cari Luna, and K.L.Pereira. And to my fellow students in these classes who read and commented so generously, thank you for your enthusiasm and ideas. Thanks as well to my original writing group, Mary, Harley, Siri, and Jenn, who read and commented on early drafts of all these stories; I so appreciate your efforts. And to my most recent writing group, even in the zoom world, thank you Sylvia, Nancy, and Rebecca, wonderful writers all, for your inspiring suggestions on how to grow these stories.

To all the gardeners, past and present, who keep these amazing gardens alive and changing through the many centuries, my gratitude and respect and wonder.

To Simon, who helps me garden, thank you!

And to Bruce, who helps me with everything, every day, I am so fortunate.

ABOUT THE AUTHOR

Arlene MacLeod was born in Massachusetts and grew up in New England and upstate New York. She earned her undergraduate degree from Bowdoin College, where she studied government and history, and she holds a Ph.D from Yale University in Political Science. She taught comparative politics and political theory at Bates College, where her courses combined her interests in literature, politics, and imagination. She lives with her husband near the coast in Maine, where she enjoys long walks, swimming in the ocean, and painting. She has always loved to read, especially books that transport the reader to a different time and place. She is the author of two novels, *A Necessary Garden* and *Far Other Worlds*, and with her son Morgan MacLeod, of *Ruins*, a collection of short stories and photo essays.

WWW.ARLENEMACLEOD.COM